The Air Merchant

Alexander Belyaev

Translation and cover art by Maria K. with images provided by
123RF
Editing by Virginia Woods Roberts

*****

PUBLISHED BY:

TSK Group LLC
THE AIR MERCHANT

Copyright © 2016 by TSK Group LLC

TABLE OF CONTENTS

I.   CURSED COUNTRY 1

II.   THE "DEAD KAYAK"..8

III.   AY-TOYON'S NOSTRIL 17

IV.   AN UNEXPECTED MEETING 24

V.   FROM THE SKY TO A LECTURE 31

VI.   THE UNDERGROUND CITY.....................................38

VII.   AN UNSUCCESSFUL ESCAPE 43

VIII.   "MISTER FATUM" 49

IX.   "THE ROYAL PARDON"..55

X.   AN UNDERGROUND JOURNEY 61

XI.   PRISONERS OF THE UNDERGROUND CITY 75

XII.   A NEW ACQUAINTANCE...85

XIII.   CALM BEFORE THE STORM 91

XIV.   MR. KLIMENKO'S "TRICKS" 98

XV.   THE WORLD SUFFOCATES... 104

XVI.   THE GAME BEGINS..110

XVII.   EXPLOSIVE DEMONSTRATION...........................118

XVIII.   BAILEY TAKES OFF HIS MASK 125

XIX.   HANDS UNTIED...130

XX.   DOOMED 138

XXI.   "MERCHANT WENT BUST" 147

ABOUT THE AUTHOR...153

ABOUT THE TRANSLATOR 157

I. CURSED COUNTRY

"Cursed country!" was how writer V. G. Korolenko described Turukhansk Region. However, this description is also applicable to Yakutia. Miserable, sparse plant life... Sickly cedars, ashes, and birches in places protected from the wind... Further to the north – bushes, seemingly twisted by sickness, creeping birch, dwarf alders and heather; even further – swamps and moss. Whenever you look at these frail, dejected trees and bushes helplessly clinging to the ground, it seems as if the poor plants want to dive underground, hide from the icy wind, and no longer see the "cursed country" they ended up in by the cruel twist of fate. Had it been up to them, they would have pulled their twisted roots out of the frozen soil and crawled to the south, toward the beneficent sun, warmth, and gentle breezes. But the trees are forced to die where they were born; all they can do is bow lower under the strikes of the wind and await their doom.

Man, however, is different – he picks his own path and his own fate, leaves the sun, warmth, and comfort, drawn by his longing for struggle to the strange, inhospitable lands, to triumph over nature or leave his bones in the cold ground under a sickly, crooked birch.

Such were the somewhat gloomy thoughts that popped into my mind, as my guide and assistant, Yakut Nikola, and I made our way along the shore of the Yana River. The main base of our expedition was located in the capital of Yakutia – Verkhoyansk, a small town with a population that could fit into a Moscow apartment building of average size.

1

Verkhoyansk remained largely the same as it was many years ago – a few dozen wooden houses, largely without permanent roofs, and just as many yurts scattered in no particular pattern along the Yana's shores, in a swampy lowland scattered with large lakes. Almost every house had its "personal" lake in front of it, but the water was polluted and unfit for drinking, and people living there had to stock up on ice year-round. Only the signs for government offices, stores, and cooperatives suggested the city's early steps toward modern age.

I left all my complex, expensive equipment in Verkhoyansk – Richar's barographs, microbarographs, anemometers, and barometers. All I had with me were a small barometer, thermometer, and a rather primitive weather wand – a source of Nikola's great enjoyment. He found it as amusing as a child's whirligig.

The expedition I was leading was organized for the purpose of studying the climatic conditions around the pole of cold located in the vicinity of Verkhoyansk, primarily to determine the reason of wind direction changes in the area.

Some time earlier, meteorologists had established an odd phenomenon – trade winds and monsoons started changing their direction. In the equatorial zone, winds normally blowing from the east toward the equator started deviating toward the north. The further northward, the more noticeable this deviation became. Synoptic maps revealed a kind of apex having formed in the Verkhoyansk Region, where the winds converged like rays of light in an enormous focal point. This resulted in a slight, albeit barely noticeable change in the average temperature – downward around the equator and upward in the north. This phenomenon was understandable, considering the cold winds from the South Pole were now drawn toward the equator, and the warm equatorial winds – to the north. There were other odd phenomena registered only by precise instruments and a few engineers overseeing pneumatic equipment operations. Their observations indicated a small drop in atmospheric pressure. The same was confirmed by a decrease in sound volume, especially at higher altitudes (pilots flying at the height of two thousand meters mistook them for engine failure.)

Apparently, most people and animals felt or noticed nothing dangerous or harmful in these meteorological changes, but scientists, ever-watchful near their instruments, were uneasy. Without raising a general alarm, they took measures to determine reasons of these strange phenomena. I was honored to be selected to participate in this work.

While the supply manager wrapped up the preparations in Verkhoyansk and purchased horses and sled dogs, I decided to set out on foot to get a better idea about our route. In these latitudes, the winds blew from west to east so strongly and evenly, even my basic instruments made it possible to pinpoint our location with reasonable precision. Our path lay toward an offshoot of the Verkhoyansk Ridge.

My guide and companion Nikola was a typical Yakut. He had long, thin arms, short, bandy legs, and was somewhat sluggish and heavy in his movements. His ideal mode of existence was to do nothing, eat a lot, and grow fat. Despite this dubious ideal, he was an excellent, diligent worker and a tireless walker. Nature had blessed him with great cheerfulness – Nikola would have never survived in the "cursed country" without it. Although, the country wasn't at all cursed to him. As far as he was concerned, Yakutia was the best place on Earth, and Nikola would not have traded his mosses and twisted birches for all the luxuriant palm trees of the south.

He often smoked his little wooden pipe or hummed songs about the sun ever-present in the sky, the river, the stones, a passing bird, and anything else he encountered along the way. His dark eyes with slightly slanting lids noticed many things that slipped from my attention, despite the fact Nikola, as I learned, was partly color-blind – the colors of his native land were so sparse, he saw most of the world in much the same way as we see black-and-white movies.

"Summer very nice," he said, spitting yellow tobacco. "Very warm."

He was right – summer was uncommonly warm for Yakutia. Even at night (with the sun never setting this time of year), temperature never fell below freezing, and during the day it rose up to 85 degrees Fahrenheit, or even higher.

We crossed the river and started climbing the mountain slope overgrown with willow, larch, and dwarf birch. Despite very warm weather, we had to cross icy patches or "taryns" from time to time – entire little islands of ice. Enormous cracks left behind by savage colds covered the ground in a thick network similar to the network of wrinkles adorning Nikola's face.

We were in the middle of the "red night" – the crimson sun rolled slowly across the north, coloring crimson the tops of the snow-covered hills.

We made it across a mountain creek without any trouble, and I started looking around for a place to camp for the night, when Nikola halted, pulled the pipe from his mouth, spat, and said calmly, "Shout."

"Who is shouting?"

4

"Person."

I listened. I couldn't hear a single sound.

"I can't hear anything," I said.

"Person shout far!" Nikola waved off to the side. "Trouble, maybe."

"If there's trouble, then we have to go help. Maybe it's a hunter attacked by some animal."

"If you say. Come. Don't go hunt if don't know shoot. Don't know shoot – crow beat you up," Nikola said instructively, while sprinting up the slope.

I barely kept up with him.

We walked at least another kilometer before I finally heard a subdued human cry. Nikola had remarkably acute hearing! The shouts suddenly stopped, and I heard two muffled gun shots.

"Very fool. Shout first, shoot second. Must shoot first," Nikola grumbled.

We climbed to the top and saw a marshy clearing. The moss-covered bog was encased in rocky shores. A few meters from the bank I saw a human figure, half-stuck in the swamp.

The man must have seen us too because he started waving his arms. Jumping from rock to rock, we rushed to his help. I held out the barrel end of my rifle, and the man grabbed it with his right hand. In his left, he held an object that looked like a very muddy kerosene canister.

"Leave the jug!" Nikola shouted to the man. But the latter apparently had no intention of doing so. He grunted, rocked back and forth, strained his right arm, but continued holding his mysterious vessel in his left hand.

"Throw it to the shore!" I shouted.

The man took my advice. He took a big swing, threw the canister to the bank, grabbed the barrel with both hands, and started slowly crawling out of the silt.

It took some work for us to get the stranger all the way to the shore. I was struck by his appearance. His rather plump, clean-shaven face was clearly European. He wore a very muddy, but well-made hiking suit, and a gray cap.

Once on the shore, he first of all grabbed his canister, which was apparently very precious to him. He then held out his hand to me and said in a broken Russian, "Thank you so much. I had no hope of getting help here. Did you hear my shots?"

"Yes, your shots. Also he, Nikola, heard your cries for help."

The stranger nodded his approval at Nikola.

"My gun is lost, but that's nothing," he continued. "Your Yakut is a good man. Are you surprised? I'm a member of an expedition – sent to study the Arctic by the Royal British Geographic Society. Are you a scientist too?"

"Yes, I am from the USSR Academy of Sciences. Would you like to dry off?" I asked, still looking at him with some curiosity.

What I mistook for a canister turned out something else entirely, but I did not know what. The cylinder had a mercury-like surface, gleaming through the mud and was topped by a narrow bottle neck. Judging by the strain in the stranger's arm, it was rather heavy.

"Dry off? No, thank you. No need. Thank you."

He nodded, suddenly turned, and started quickly climbing up the slope.

I gazed after him in confusion. The man rescued from certain death could have paid us more attention. Where did he come from anyway? I'd never heard of an expedition sent here from Britain. And his strange canister...

"Very fool. Left pistol, saved jug," Nikola expressed his opinion about the stranger.

He then thought about something, shook his head in disapproval, and started gathering dried branches for our fire. We were both soaking wet after our rescue mission.

"Hey! Hey!" I suddenly heard the stranger's voice. He was standing on a large mossy rock and waving at us.

"A return favor!" the Englishman shouted. "Don't go that way." He pointed downwind. "You'll die!" He nodded, jumped off the rock, and vanished.

What a strange warning! I thought. *Not to go downwind?* But that was exactly where I needed to go. I had to investigate the focal point where winds from all over the globe seemed to be drawn.

II.   THE "DEAD KAYAK"

As soon as we stopped, we were swathed in a cloud of gnats. Apparently, this was nothing compared to what was common around here in the summer.

"Very not enough gnats though," Nikola said. "Wind blows off."

"Not enough!" I grumbled.

"Must be very more. Can't see sun, can't see mountain – this many. Must have this many gnat," Nikola replied, starting the fire and setting our camp kettle on a tripod made of branches.

While we waited for the water to boil, Nikola lit his pipe, stretched out on the ground, and pondered something. He was unusually quiet, not singing and not singing. The silence continued for some time. The Nikola exhaled a thick stream of smoke and said, "Too bad though. Too bad." Nikola was clearly preoccupied by something.

"What's bad, Nikola?" I asked him.

"That man. Too bad. Let him drown. Three times summer, three times winter – I saw such man."

"You know him?" I asked Nikola in surprise.

"Not him. Like him. There!" Nikola pointed to the north.

"Stop talking in riddles, Nikola," I said impatiently. "What's the matter?"

Nikola told me a strange story in his broken Russian, poor in vocabulary but rich in images and spot-on descriptions.

This was three years earlier. Nicola, his father, and brother were fishing in the Sellakh Bay. Summer was drawing to its end. The wind was blowing from the shore, but icebergs appearing in the Northern Sea with increasing frequency spoke

8

of the approaching winter. Nikola suggested going home sooner, but the catch was good, and Nikola's father, an old experienced fisherman, refused to hurry. He argued the frost would be accompanied by northern wind, which was bound to carry them to the shore.

The dying summer, however, refused to surrender to winter without a battle. Southern wind strengthened and grew into a storm. The fishermen drifted toward the Island of Makar. Their small sail was torn off, and their rudder broke against an iceberg. Grizzled waves shoved the little kayak around like a woodchip. Accustomed to the dangers of his trade, the fishermen kept their spirits high. The ice floes provided them with fresh water, and they had plenty of fish. It was cold, but they grew up in the coldest place on Earth. Their organisms resisted. Half-frozen, covered in ice, they encouraged each other with jokes.

The disaster happened on the third day of their ordeal – their kayak became trapped between two icebergs and was crushed like an egg. The fishermen barely managed to climb out onto an ice floe and continued traveling on it.

The prediction made by Nikola's father came true, albeit with some delay – the shore wind subsided, and soon they felt the sustained icy breath from the north. The ice floe turned toward the shore, but it was too far. Hunger was becoming a serious problem for the survivors. They had lost all their fish with the kayak. Fishing by hand wasn't an easy task. The fishermen were becoming weak with hunger. The sea roiled, stirred up by the change in the wind. Icy spray showered the travelers from head to toe. Sometimes, waves rolled over their heads.

"Very bad it was, almost dead," Nikola explained.

The white nights were over, and the sun did disappear beyond the horizon, but the nights were still very light. One such night the fishermen saw a "very big kayak" moving directly at them in the halo of bright lights.

It was a steam ship – the biggest Nikola had ever seen. The fishermen shouted and waved. The ship approached, but they saw no people. Since it was moving directly toward the ice floe, the fishermen decided they had been noticed. *Why no sound?* Nikola thought. The closer the ship came, the bigger it seemed. "Had to look like so," Nikola explained, turning his face toward the sky.

The fishermen's joy soon gave way to horror. The bow of the enormous ship was only a few meters away, and they still didn't see a single person on deck. A moment later the ship's keel ran into the ice floe and split it in half. There was a terrible crackling, Nikola was doused with icy water and felt the ice floe slipping out from under his feet. When Nikola surfaced, his father and brother were gone. They ended up on the half of the ice floe to the left side of the ship, and Nikola was on the left. Nikola never saw his father or brother again and did not know what happened to them.

Nikola splashed in the water, as the metal wall of the ship's hull sailed by him. There was no doubt – the ship's crew did not notice them. Nikola was doomed if he did nothing to save himself. Water pressure pushed Nikola away from the ship, but he was a good swimmer and, through incredible effort, managed to stay close. Lit port holes glided past Nikola. He shouted, but no one appeared.

Suddenly, Nikola saw the end of a cable dangling from the deck. His shoulder joints almost popping out of their sockets, Nikola moved toward the cable, but a wave pushed him aside, and he passed the cable when it was only a couple of feet away from his hand. Nikola was becoming desperate. But he wasn't destined to die that day after all. Soon he saw a rope ladder hanging almost to the water. Nikola jumped up and reached for the ladder. The Ice floe turned over under him, but he was already on the ladder. He was safe. Nikola quickly climbed the ladder and made it to the deck, expecting to see surprised sailors.

However, it wasn't sailors who were surprised but Nikola himself – the deck was empty. There wasn't a single person there. A dead ship! The only sound was the muffled hum of the powerful engines.

Nikola had never heard the legend of the Flying Dutchman, but the poor Yakut was overcome with the same terror as those who had encountered the legendary ship.

He was so frightened he considered jumping off. The sight of the stormy ocean brought him to his senses.

Maybe people afraid of cold. Maybe inside, he decided and examined the ship, climbing up and down ladders and sneaking down hallways as carefully as a ship. All the passenger quarters were empty, including the captain's quarters; the cabin, the cockpit, and the galley were deserted.

Nikola went from being terrified to being confused. If everyone died, there should have been at least a few corpses of those who survived longer than others. If everyone fled, how was the ship still running? If it was running, then the mechanic, the stoker, and the navigator should have been around.

Nikola went down to the boiler room, but no one was there. The engine room was also empty. The ship traveled, seemingly guided by a ghost. Nikola felt his hair standing on end from horror. Beside himself with fear, he returned above deck and made his way to the steering wheel. No one! Propelled by terror, Nikola ran to the ship's bow. He finally saw someone – a man standing by the railing and looking down.

"Hey! It's me! Who are you?" Nikola shouted in a hoarse voice.

The man remained motionless. He was as scary as everything else on that ship, but Nikola felt such need to see at least one living being he overcame his fear, walked up to the man, and looked into his face. The man was dead! Only now did he see the body was tied to the railing with a thin rope.

Based on Nikola's description, the dead man was much like the Englishman we pulled out from the swamp – he too was clean-shaven and dressed the same way. I now understood Nikola's gloomy mood – our encounter reminded him of the most tragic event in his life.

"What happened after you saw the dead man?"

"I howled. Like wolf," Nikola replied.

He continued his story. Nikola had never seen anything more terrifying than the "dead kayak" in his entire life. But at least the ship was warm and dry. His hunger surpassed his fear, and Nikola set out in search of provisions. He found several barrels of fresh water, although the food situation was somewhat worse. Nikola managed to find a sack of crackers stashed behind some empty crates. For the undemanding Yakut even that little bit was a good find.

Dead people drink water and don't eat; Nikola decided and stuffed the first cracker into his mouth with some trepidation. He was afraid a dead arm would suddenly appear from behind his back and the corpse would scream, "Give back my crackers!"

But the dead turned out to be very obliging and didn't keep Nikola from eating a dozen crackers and drinking two ladles of water.

When Nikola had a chance to eat and dry himself, he felt a great deal better. He picked a comfortable room, praised the dead for their kindness just in case, and stretched out on the soft mattress. His last thought was the ship must have been sent for him by some guardian spirit. It was awful his brother and father perished, but such was life – some lived, some died!

Nikola fell soundly asleep and slept for a very long time. He was woken up by screeching, cracking, and rocking of the ship. When he opened his eyes, Nikola couldn't recall what had happened to him and where he was. Finally remembering he was in the "dead kayak", he jumped out of bed. Something odd must have been happening to the ship – it was as if the dead returned and were dancing, their bones rattling. Nikola became frightened once again. He climbed above deck. Powerful, brutal, icy wind almost knocked him off his feet. The ship was rocking. Nikola looked ahead and was dumbstruck with horror. Enormous icebergs danced, collided, and shattered around the ship, rumbling, and screeching. But that wasn't what scared Nikola the most. Picked up by a strong current, the ship was flying along the narrow gulf between two sheer rock walls, heading toward another wall. The dead played a bad trick on Nikola, and he no longer thought the ship had been dispatched by a guardian spirit.

Nikola ran up to the dead man tied to the bow, grabbed his shoulder, and shook him so hard, as if trying to shake some life out of him.

"What you doing? See?" Nikola shouted. "Turn back!"

The corpse fell forward, and his cap rolled overboard. He didn't listen to Nikola, and the ship continued to rush toward the rock. Nikola dashed to the wheel, but quickly realized it would be no help, since the gulf was too narrow. With the last glimmer of hope, Nikola ran into the cockpit and shouted into the horn connected to the engine room, "Back up!" like the ship's captain he saw on the river Lena.

The mechanic's spirit refused to obey. The engine continued humming.

"Very fools!" Nikola scolded his imaginary companions.

He was used to making decisions quickly. Seeing all his efforts to avoid the catastrophe were in vain, he did everything he had time for to save himself. He rushed below deck, grabbed the sack of crackers, threw it into a boat, and climbed in himself to wait for further developments. They didn't keep him waiting. The ship hit the rock with such force, Nikola was thrown onto the deck along with the boat. The terrible snapping sound from the collision was drowned out by the even more terrible roar of the exploded boilers. The ship started sinking. It rolled to one side, and the waves swept across the deck. Nikola took this opportunity and dragged the boat into the water.

Whirlpools spun the boat around, and the ice floes got in the way of the oars. The ship might have dragged the boat with it. It was a very dangerous moment. But Nikola gradually made it away from the ship, keeping an eye on it all the time, and finally ended up in a current flowing around the rock. His boat sailed quickly along the sheer drop and turned around the corner, before the shop sunk in the midst of a terrible whirlpool.

Nikola was saved. Two days later, he made it to the Island of Makar and then, across the ice – to the shore.

Nikola finished the story of his odyssey and started thoughtfully sharpening a stick, using his knife with a mammoth bone hilt carved in the shape of a deer head. Nikola was a very skilled bone carver.

I too had something to think about. The story about the "dead kayak" was so unusual it felt made up. But I knew Nikola – he might have exaggerated a few details but he was not a liar. A sudden thought came to my mind.

"What was the name of that ship?" I asked Nikola. He smacked his lips in response and shook his head.

"Did you see the inscription on the life preservers? Can't you recall at least the first letter? What did it look like?"

Nikola thought about it and said, "Like a tripod for the teapot." With his knife he drew a figure similar to letter A.

Was my theory correct?

I recalled that three years earlier, an expedition was dispatched from Britain. It was financed by a wealthy businessman, Mr. Bailey, and traveled on an icebreaker *Arctic*. The expedition was wonderfully equipped with every necessity and planned to travel along the entire coast of Siberia, all the way to Alaska. There were several well-known scientists on board.

However, the expedition ended tragically. The last radio transmissions were received when the ship was not far from Cape Borkhai. There was no news from *Arctic* for several days, and then there were several SOS messages. There was nothing else. The next year, fishing vessels found two shattered boats from the icebreaker on one of the small barren islands. A life preserver from *Arctic* surfaced in the delta of the Lena. It must have been all that's left of the ship. The brave explorers were added to the long list of the fallen soldiers of science, and *Arctic* was written off. That was all.

And now, in the "cursed country", from the lips of a Yakut, I heard a story shedding some light on the icebreaker's fate but, at the same time, surrounding it in an even greater mystery. Where were its passengers? How did the ship end up traveling across the ocean full speed without a crew? The engines could not have worked without the crew. The boiler ought to have exploded or cooled without fuel, and the ship should have stopped.

Who was the Englishman we rescued from the swamp? He said he was a member of a science expedition. But he didn't look like a man who survived a shipwreck several years earlier and had to survive in one of the harshest corners of the globe. Besides, what was the meaning of his warning? Why was in danger if I followed the wind? There was a mystery in that warning. Well, he wasn't going to frighten me! Our expedition's mission was to follow the wind.

In any case, I had to be careful. Good sense suggested I return to Verkhoyansk and return to investigate with the entire group. Had I listened to it, many things would have been different. Resisting my own caution, I assured myself I would only walk another few kilometers to look for the signs of danger possibly awaiting me.

"Tea ready," Nikola said, taking the boiling kettle off the tripod.

III.   AY-TOYON'S NOSTRIL

Tired by our journey, we fell soundly asleep, having wrapped our heads against the gnats. When Nikola woke me, the never-setting sun had moved toward the east. It was morning. The wind, having somewhat subsided overnight, was once again hard at work. It blew evenly, without gusts, with increasing strength.

"Let's go that way," I said, pointing downwind.

A mountain range was before us.

"That way again? Nikola asked, clearly somewhat alarmed. "Go back. I won't go."

I was surprised by his answer. Nikola – fearless and diligent Nikola was refusing to continue our journey! Was he frightened by the Englishman's words?

"Why won't you go there?" I asked.

"One friend and another friend went and didn't come back," Nikola said, frowning. "No one comes back. That's Ay-Toyon's nostril."

I knew Ay-Toyon was the "holy man" – the Yakut's highest deity. But I'd never heard about Ay-Toyon's nostril.

"Do you really believe all this nonsense about Ay-Toyon? How can you be scared? I'm coming with you."

"I know, you very big man. Bolshevik. But no one comes back."

Nikola wasn't flattering me by calling me a "very big man" and a Bolshevik. As far as he was concerned, anyone coming from a large city had to be a Bolshevik. His praise was sincere. The new government freed him and other Yakuts from the exploitation of merchants who bought valuable furs for pennies and bribed the Yakuts with vodka. Nikola's children now went to school, and his wife had been cured from an illness he believed to have been sent by an evil spirit "yer". This was the kind of factual motivation Nikola could understand and appreciate. Whenever he encountered doubt about divine powers, his faith in them was shaken. I thought Nikola was gradually losing that faith and treated his deities as poetic fantasies, generalizing various phenomena – just as we spoke of "fortune" or "Nemesis", forgetting about religious origins of these words and using them to communicate ordinary, everyday notions. Nikola's gods have been rotting for a long time but were yet to die off entirely in his mind. They came alive whenever he encountered something strange and frightening. This happened to him on the dead ship, and it was happening again. Fear drowned out the voice of reason and awakened primeval beliefs in evil spirits.

"What is this Ay-Toyon's nostril?"

"Simple nostril. Ay Toyon is breathing. Over there," Nikola pointed at the mountain, "is his nostril."

"Why does he breathe in without breathing out? See, the wind is blowing in the same direction?" I asked Nikola.

"Ay-Toyon very big. Breathe in a thousand years, breathe out another thousand."

Apparently, I was witnessing the birth of a new legend.

"It's nonsense! Come with me, Nikola, and you'll see there's no nostril."

But Nikola didn't move and shook his head.

"Are you coming?"

"Very scared. You don't go, though!" he said. I hesitated. Going alone would be risky. The Englishman said what he did for a good reason. There really might have been some unforeseen dangers ahead. But I was suddenly overcome with pride. Nikola might have mistaken my hesitation for believing the stupid story about the nostril.

"If you refuse, I'm going alone!" I said firmly and headed up the slope. The wind was blowing at my back, making my climb easier.

"Don't go!" Nikola shouted. "Don't go!"

I ignored him and kept climbing.

The slope became steeper and steeper. Soon, I started feeling tired and slowed down. I paused before the hardest part of the climb to catch my breath and suddenly heard someone's huffing behind my back. I turned and saw Nikola. He was smiling with his big mouth, baring his crooked teeth.

"You go, I go, though," he said, seeing my confusion.

"Good man, Nikola!" I said happily. I had to shout. The wind wailed and whistled so loudly we could barely hear each other.

"Aren't you scared, Nikola?"

"Very scared, though. Come!"

We continued climbing. Soon the wind pulled off my portable weather wane, which was strapped behind my back. Nikola tried going after it but I stopped him. The wind blew with such persistence; there was no need for a wane. Nikola, however, might have fallen into a crevasse, propelled by this insane wind.

"Come here! Hold on to me! Let's go together!" I shouted to the Yakut.

We clutched at each other and continued, helping one another up the slope. We had to lean back a lot and still had a hard time keeping our footing. We kept falling down and getting up with difficulty. The wind pressed against our backs like heavy sacks with sand. We sweated buckets and were losing our strength. I was beginning to regret my rash decision, but I didn't want to go back. We weren't far from the peak, and I promised myself to just look what was going on to the other side of the ridge and go back without tempting fates any further. We crossed the small distance between us and the peak at a crawl. The wind seemed to be ready to crush us like slugs. It was dense and heavy. It was as if we were at the bottom of the ocean, being crushed by hundreds of tons of water. We had to cover our mouths and noses to keep in the air we breathed in and breathed out with great difficulty, like asthma patients.

I knew the wind would be even wilder at the crest. To keep from being blown off into some canyon, I took some safety measures. I found a crack between the rocks and headed that way to move along behind the granite outcroppings.

We crawled along this narrow gap without any trouble. The crack turned at a sharp angle and finally took us to the top. I tipped my head and looked down. The sight before me was astonishing.

I saw an enormous sloping crater, like something from Lunar surface. What was particularly surprising was the seemingly polished slopes of this enormous crater. There wasn't a single rock or bump to be seen. It was a completely smooth, shallow funnel. Far below, in its center, was a round hole of tremendous dimensions. Could the polished funnel and the geometrically perfect opening at the bottom of the crater be of natural origin? I couldn't believe that.

Holding on to a sharp bit of rock, Nikola waved to point something out and shouted, but I couldn't hear him and looked in the direction he was pointing. I saw a tree flying through the air along an enormous circle following the edge of the crater, as if carried by whirlwind. We watched the tree. It continued circling or, rather, spiraling – each circle was smaller and lower than the previous. The tree's speed increased. It was a true atmospheric Maelstrom. The tree made a few more circles and vanished in the black well at the bottom of the crater.

I was faced with a new riddle. It was clear the air was moving into the ground. This was as incomprehensible and meaningless as Ay-Toyon's nostril.

But where's the other nostril to let the air out?

My thoughts were interrupted by a new phenomenon. An enormous boulder, at least a ton in weight, suddenly broke away from the mountain top. But it didn't fly down, as one might expect. It flew through the air along a spiral two-thirds the diameter of the crater before it reached the bottom.

What's the wind power up there? I wondered and shuddered despite myself, imagining myself in place of that rock.

We were faced with an exceptional, mysterious natural phenomenon. While I didn't believe in some monstrous nostril, I considered Nikola's myth-making with greater regard. There was a dose of truth in his tale – we have discovered some monstrous "nostril" in the Earth's crust, sucking the air from the surface.

This is bound to create a sensation in the science world! I had a vain thought. This, however, was neither the time nor the place to indulge in such thoughts. I had to consider how we would get out of this air funnel. With utmost caution, I freed one arm, touched Nikola's shoulder and nodded to the side, inviting him to go back.

Why doesn't this hole get plugged up with trash? I thought. At that moment, something happened and knocked all other thoughts out of my head.

Nikola moved his hands too quickly and carelessly, and his body suddenly started sliding off the ledge, on which we were stretched under the pressure from the dense air masses. I barely managed to grab Nikola's feet and felt with horror I too was being pulled to the edge. I tried hooking the toes of my boots into small dents in the rock to slow down our movement, but all was in vain – we slowly, inexorably moved toward the edge of the abyss. Nikola's body was already half-hanging in the air. The wind blew the sack off his back. The sack was still attached by its straps and hung horizontally in front of Nikola's head. A moment later, Nikola's entire body hung over the crater. I felt him pulling his legs, as if trying to free himself from my grip. I didn't understand him. Nikola turned his head toward me with some difficulty and shouted, "Let go!"

He was a loyal friend and a real man. Faced with certain death, he wanted to at least allow me to save myself. I couldn't accept his sacrifice and continued holding his feet. Nikola's body stretched out. The sack with food, tea pot, and instruments pulled away and flew off to the left, along the edge of the enormous funnel. At the same moment, Nikola pulled his legs so hard I let go. Nikola flew after the sack at an insane speed, as if trying to catch up to it. In a moment my own body followed Nikola's.

These were terrible, unforgettable moments! The first thing I felt was the wind had subsided – we were now traveling with it. At the same time, I felt unusual increase in the density of the surrounding air, as if I, once again, was at the bottom of the ocean. With great difficulty, I spread my arms to try and grab the edge of the crater. I was flying only a meter away from it. Breathing was a bit easier. Turning my head, I looked at Nikola flying ahead of me. He too apparently tried to catch the edge of the crater. Despite his usual sluggishness, he writhed like a worm, reaching with his long arms, and spreading his legs. For one moment, he managed to touch the stone wall with one foot. But this didn't halt his flight and only slowed it down. His body flipped over and drifted closer to me. He once again stretched out flat, and I reached out, trying to grab him. Even if there was no more than a centimeter between us, I couldn't have gotten to him, because the distance between us remained constant. We were helpless to do anything else.

The sack had made a full circle and was now flying a little lower than the ledge, from which we fell. Nikola followed the sack, as did I. Closer up the wall of the crater, it didn't seem quite as smooth as from the distance. There were cracks, dents, and outcroppings. But it was impossible to grab them. Even if I succeeded, my arm would have been torn off by the raging flow, like a fly's leg. I had to surrender to my fate and await what would happen next.

Nikola and I looked down to see what was waiting for us. There was a round black hole, growing in size as we came closer to it following our spiraling route in the air, flying faster and faster in smaller circles.

I was becoming woozy. The circles were shrinking; we were falling deeper and deeper. I was certain we were about to die, and our death was unavoidable. I was about to fall into the abyss and crash against the rocks somewhere far below. When we flew over the opening, I summoned my strength to look down. Perhaps I was delusional, but I thought I saw the light from enormous electric lamps and a grate below. The grate spun suddenly, the lights went out, and I fainted.

IV.   AN UNEXPECTED MEETING

The first thing I felt when I regained consciousness was my sore and aching body. Before I opened my eyes, I felt someone's touch. Forcing my eyelids open, I saw my faithful companion and friend Nikola. I didn't recognize him right away. Instead of his usual garb made of deer skins, he was dressed in a gray hospital robe.

I was in a clean, neatly made bed, covered with a fluffy gray blanket, in a small room without windows, lit by an electric lamp hanging from the ceiling.

"We are here!" Nikola said, greeting me with his usual smile.

"In Ay-Toyon's nostril?" I tried joking. "See, Nikola, there's no nostril."

"Did you see? Maybe that's how nostril is." Nikola pointed at the room.

"With electric lights?!"

Our conversation was interrupted. The door opened, and a young woman in a white coat came in – I decided she was a nurse. I had no doubt I was in a hospital. I had no idea how long I'd been unconscious or how I avoided death and ended up in this hospital.

The nurse addressed me with a question in a language I didn't know. I gestured I didn't understand her while studying her face. She was young, rosy-cheeked, and very healthy. A lock of blond hair escaped from under her white cap. She smiled flashing even, white teeth, and repeated the question in English. I was more familiar with it – I could read in English, but didn't speak it. I spread my hands. Then the girl repeated her question for the third time, in German.

24

"How do you feel?" she asked.

"Very well, thank you," I replied although, to be honest, I didn't feel very well at all.

"Anything hurts?"

"What doesn't hurt? I feel as if I'd been through a bunch of grinding stones," I replied.

"Could have been worse," the girl said with a good-natured smile.

"Would you be so kind as to tell me where I am?" I asked.

"You'll find out soon enough. Can you get up?"

I tried and bit my lip from pain.

"Stay where you are, I'll bring your breakfast." She left, stepping noiselessly in her soft shoes.

Nikola was feeling better than I. He kept rubbing his side and his back, but he was up and about. He paced around the small room, grunting and holding on to his right knee.

"Pipe gone, tobacco gone, want to smoke," he said.

The door opened again, and the nurse returned accompanied by a man of about thirty, clean-shaven and dressed in a wool jacket and boots made of horse skins. This suggested we were still somewhere around the polar circle. The man was carrying similar outfits for Nikola and me. The nurse held a breakfast tray with fried eggs, toast, and steaming cups of cocoa.

"Enjoy," she said kindly, "and when you feel well enough to get up, get dressed, and ring this bell."

She nodded to the man, and the two of them left the room. I tucked into the fried eggs set on the small table by my bed. Despite our tribulations, Nikola and I enjoyed our breakfast. Nikola had never had cocoa and found it a source of great enjoyment. He even closed his eyes and smacked his lips as he sipped the hot beverage.

Apparently, one wasn't expected to stay bedridden very long at this hospital. Having finished my breakfast, I struggled to my feet and examined my body. I'd been bathed by someone and dressed into clean underwear. I was covered in numerous bruises but no bones were broken. My right shoulder was swollen and ached a lot. It looked like I popped the right shoulder joint, and someone had to set it. Yes, could have been worse...

Nikola and I got dressed, helping each other, and I pressed the call button by the door. Soon, the man in the wool jacket came back and gestured for us to follow him.

We left the room and set out down a long, arching hallway lit by electric lamps. There were numbered doors on both sides: 32, 33, 34.... And 12, 13, 14 across from them, like in a hotel or a government building.

We walked for some time, the hallway curving to the side. A constant, even hum came from somewhere. Some huge machines were working somewhere around here. No, this was more like a factory!

Our guide suddenly halted by door 1 and knocked. We entered a large office, beautifully furnished and decorated with rugs. I noticed there were no windows. The walls were hung with technical drawings and lined with book cases. There was a safe in the corner, a large Swedish office desk, and next to it – a spinning étagère with folders. At the desk lit by a lamp with a green shade sat a clean-shaven man, writing something. A phone rang. The man at the desk picked it up.

"Hello!" and then he gave a quick order in a strange language.

He then leaned back in his revolving chair and turned to face us. He was dressed in a gray jacket and a gray wool vest with a V-neck revealing a dress shirt and a plaid tie. I felt as if we were in an office of a wealthy factory director. Having finished studying his suit, I looked at the foreigner's face and gasped in surprised. It was the Englishman we rescued from the swamp.

He too was clearly surprised by our meeting.

"Ah, old friends!" he said. "Sit."

We sat down by the desk. For a minute, the Englishman looked at us as if pondering something, then shook his head in disapproval, knocked a drafting triangle against the desk, and said, "You didn't listen to my advice after all."

"But we are alive," I said, trying to appear at ease.

"For now!" the Englishman said meaningfully. "It's pure accident you weren't shattered like eggshells."

He drummed his fingers on the table, then turned away and became absorbed in some papers, as if forgetting about us. A rather tiresome pause followed. Then he turned to face us again just as abruptly.

"Those who follow the wind don't come back!" he snapped, repeating what Nikola said to me once. "Either they die before they get here, or... But you saved my life. I am in your debt, and I do not wish you to die. But..." The Englishman raised his finger. He then half-turned, wrote something on a piece of paper, and asked, "Who are you and what is your name?"

"Klimenko, Georgy Pavlovich. And this is Nikola." The Englishman carefully wrote down my answers as if he was a detective. He asked my age, job title, education, and purpose of my expedition (the latter was of the utmost interest to him.) I considered it unnecessary to hide anything from him.

27

"May I ask, to whom I have the honor addressing?" I ask to equalize our situation somehow. The Englishman snorted and said, "You may. You have the honor of addressing Mr. Bailey."

"Mr. Bailey?" I asked in surprise, "the one who financed the *Arctic* expedition? You didn't die?"

"I did – as far as anyone living upwind is concerned. But, as you see... Listen, Mr. Kalimenko—"

"Klimenko," I corrected.

But Mr. Bailey couldn't seem to get my last name right, and he repeated it the same way, "You, Mr. Kalimenko, will not leave here. You too are now dead to anyone living upwind. You are a meteorologist – that is good. You will be of some use to me. I must make certain your friends don't come looking for you."

"That's impossible. As soon as they discover I disappeared, they'll dispatch a group to look for me."

"Oh, you are very fond of looking for those lost!" Bailey said with some irony. He paused. "Your own and others – Nobile, Kulik, Gorski..."

I was surprised. Apparently, Bailey was well informed about everything happening "upwind", that is, around the world. He must have had a radio station.

"Yes, we try not to leave behind people in need of help," I replied with some heat.

"Very well," Bailey said with the same sarcasm. "But we'll set things up in a way you won't need any help. Don't worry. I told you, I plan to spare your life. But I could take the clothes you were traveling in, tear it up, cover it in blood, and leave it in the path of those looking for you. You may have been attacked by wild animals. Of course! The rescue group will turn back. I don't want anyone else coming here. You may go," Bailey concluded, suddenly turning to Nikola.

When Nikola left the room, Mr. Bailey rose, walked across the office, and said, "I need to talk to you some more."

"I need to speak with you as well," I replied, still trying to even things out, if that was at all possible between the prisoner I was, and the man who held my life in his hands.

Before Bailey could speak, I continued, "You said you didn't want anyone to discover your existence or the way to get here. It's impossible. Suppose you manage to stage my death. But scientific exploration will not stop. I don't know what you are doing here, but it's clear you have caused the change in the wind direction and, thus, some changes in climate. Presently, the public is not very concerned, but scientists all around the world have been watching these strange phenomena with some anxiety for a long time. Sooner or later, everyone will feel the drop in the atmospheric pressure. Others will follow the wind and invariably arrive here."

"I know all that," Bailey replied, having listened to me with some impatience. "It is bound to happen sooner or later. They'll come here and—all the worse for them! And you! I'd already warned you once, but you didn't listen. Here is another warning – don't try escaping from here. It might cost your life. I will not spare you the second time. Tell that to your Yakut. Understand? I shall give you some freedom, if you give me your word. Although, that won't be necessary – you'll see for yourself, it's impossible to escape. You'll have a lot of work. Now go, Mr. Kalimenko. William will show you to your room."

Bailey rang. A servant entered.

"William, please take Mr. Kalimenko to the room number sixty-six. Good bye!"

"May Nikola be my roommate?" I asked.

Mr. Bailey thought about it.

"I think so," he said. "But remember, no scheming. Good bye!"

I bowed and followed William along the long sweeping hallway. We went down to a lower story and entered a real labyrinth of hallways and doors. I was surprised we didn't meet a single person along the way. I asked my guide where everyone was, but he said nothing. Maybe he didn't speak Russian or German, or maybe he didn't want to say anything.

V.   FROM THE SKY TO A LECTURE

I entered my "prison cell". The room was about thirty square meters with four-meter ceiling. The walls were covered with plywood. There was a lamp hanging from the ceiling and another one set on the desk. Two narrow beds by the walls and several plain chairs.

After Mr. Bailey's splendid office, this room felt more than modest. But… "could have been worse," I recalled the nurse's words and didn't feel too bad. William left, and my attention was soon drawn by a big drawing covering half the wall.

On the blue drafting paper, I saw the rendering of Mr. Bailey's underground city and plans of each level. There were no explanatory notes on the drawings, but they provided a reasonable impression of the structure. The center of the city was taken up by the enormous tube we fell into. Numbered rooms were located around this tube. The settlement had five levels below ground level and three more levels behind the walls of the crater. Under the eighth level were two caves, apparently natural in origin.

To the left from the central tube along the fifth level from the top, was a side tube, which ended far outside the living quarters and led to the surface. I was very interested in this tube. My first thought was that the tube was intended as an outlet for the air entering from above. However, had the same amount of air came out there as came in from the top, there would have been a second air current, and there wouldn't have been any decrease in air pressure indicated by our carefully compiled synoptic maps. Air currents from all around the globe headed to one spot, but no reverse currents were in evidence.

31

If the air went into the underground city and didn't go out, then – damn it! – why didn't the whole place explode like a boiler at high pressure?

The door opened, and Nikola came in. He carefully closed the door, scratched his head, and sighed. I expected him to reproach me for dismissing his advice, but he spoke of something else. Nikola told me he met "two Ivans" in one of the corridors – two Yakuts who had disappeared the year before somewhere around Ay-Toyon's nostril.

"Do you still believe in the nostril?" I asked him.

"I'd rather end up in the nostril than with that English 'yera'," Nikola replied worriedly.

He managed to chat briefly with the Yakuts he met and found out they worked in some big tube, removing trash brought by the wind from the central tube. I looked at the plan. So that's what the side tube was for!

The "two Ivans" complained to Nikola they were kept against their will, like slaves, never allowed to go anywhere, "but fed awfully nice".

There was a knock on the door. William returned and invited us to follow him in his language, supported by gestures.

We obeyed. Yakut Nikola knew as Ivan the Elder was standing by the door. William sent Nikola off with him, and took me down the corridor. We went across, got into the elevator 50, went up one level, and stopped by the door 13. William opened the door without knocking, and I followed him into a large room. Apparently, it was a laboratory. Complex equipment with compressors, copper tubes, spiral pipes, and cooling elements were arranged on the table in perfect order. There were entire rows of measuring cylinders, cups, and beakers. Their glossy surface shone in the bright light of two neon lamps.

The appearance of these dazzling objects was such; as if a wealthy heir pulled his grandfather's silver from a trunk to admire his treasure. But I already knew such vessels with amalgamated walls to reflect heat were used during experiments with liquid air.

Liquid air! Its density was 800 times greater than regular air. Was Bailey's underground town a factory for converting Earth's atmosphere into liquid air?

Preoccupied by my thoughts I didn't notice another person leaning over one of the tables right away. It was a woman dressed in a white coat. She looked up and I recognized the nurse I'd seen earlier. She also recognized me and smiled at the confusion on my face.

"Go ahead into the study; father is waiting for you," she said, pointing at the second door.

I knocked and went into the next room. It was almost as big as the first one, but there were no instruments. All the walls were lined with book cases, and the large desk was piled high with sheets of paper covered with chemical formulas.

A very tall, middle-aged, albeit youthful-looking man with fair hair, gray eyes, and pink cheeks rose to greet me. His kindly smile was very much like his daughter's. He firmly shook my hand and said, "Mr. Bailey and Eleonora already told me about you. We need people like you. Unfortunately, you are not a chemist, but your specialty is fairly close to mine. You make a living by studying the air, much as I do." He smiled.

He spoke so naturally, as if I came there of my own free will and was offering them my knowledge and my work.

"My name is Engelbrecht," he said. "Please, sit."

"Engelbrecht!" I exclaimed with surprise, still standing. "You are Svante Engelbrecht, whose death on board *Arctic* was mourned by the entire scientific world?"

"Rumors of my demise were significantly exaggerated," the famous Swedish scientist paraphrased the famous joke by Mark Twain. "Yes, here I am, Svante Engelbrecht, alive and well."

"But why? What made you go into hiding?"

Engelbrecht frowned.

"Please, sit down," he said. "I am Mr. Bailey's chief engineer. We produce liquid air, hydrogen, and helium, extract nitrogen and oxygen from the atmosphere."

"What do you do with them?" I couldn't help asking.

"That's Mr. Bailey's business. Apparently, he sells them..."

"But how? I don't recall hearing of any concessions..."

"I have little interest in the financial side of the matter," Engelbrecht interrupted me quickly. "You may ask Mr. Bailey about it. I am bound by my contract and do not interfere with anything, save my laboratories. Mr. Bailey is a man of great initiative and business savvy. He spares nothing to ensure I can engage in scientific work in peace and quiet. When you become familiar with it, you'll see we've made some very valuable scientific discoveries, yet unknown to the world. Mr. Bailey makes profit with them – but that is his business. I do not interfere in his financial matters," the scientist repeated once again, clearly in a hurry to tell me all I needed to know. "My only setback is the number of lab assistants. I barely have time to work on my experiments. I can conduct them only here." Engelbrecht pointed at the formula-covered sheets. "My daughter Eleonora helps me."

"The nurse?"

Engelbrecht smiled.

"She is our nurse, scientist, lab assistant, and my house keeper," he said warmly. "She is a good girl. I hope you help her with her lab work. She'll give you more information. If you have trouble with any task, let me know, I'm always happy to help, whenever necessary. Well, to our work then!" Engelbrecht, concluded holding out his hand to me. "Let's not waste any time."

I bowed and returned to the laboratory.

"Did you talk everything over?" Eleonora asked.

I spread my hands to indicate my submission to the fates.

"Have a seat and let's get to work," she said simply, pulling up a free stool.

I sat down like an obliging student. She put me through a real exam.

"The method for producing liquid air? Hm... hm... Essentially, it's a..." I began, all the while looking at locks of Eleonora's hair under her white cap, "it's a process of cooling the air by using the energy that normally maintains the air in gaseous state. The air is gradually compressed with pressure increasing to two hundred atmospheres, then the pressure suddenly drops to twenty, and the temperature – to thirty degrees below zero Celsius. This is done in several stages, until the temperature reaches minus a hundred-eighty degrees Celsius. Then, under the pressure of twenty atmospheres, the air converts to liquid state." *She has such pretty hair.* This wasn't stated out loud, of course.

Eleonora caught me staring before I managed to lower my eyes, tucked away the stray lock, smiled slightly, and said with a solemnity that didn't become her at all, "Superficial and not entirely correct, but not bad for a start. Are you familiar with this device?"

"This is Linde's device for thickening the air," I replied, as glad as a schoolboy to give the right answer. Eleonora nodded.

"Yes, but that's a child's toy compared to the complex machines my father designed." The exam continued. "You need to expand your theoretical knowledge quite a bit. Liquid air generation..." Without interrupting her work, she continued with her first lecture. I tried to focus, but my thoughts kept drifting. Presently, I was much more interested to know, how she and her father ended up in the underground settlement, what happened to the *Arctic*, who was the dead man Nikola saw on the ship, how Bailey used liquid air, and what was his relationship to the Engelbrechts. Thousands of questions roiled in my mind, but I didn't dare ask any of them of my teacher.

"Liquid air is a light, transparent liquid, pale-blue in color, liquid state temperature minus one hundred ninety-three degrees Celsius at normal pressure," Eleonora continued. "Initially, liquid air comes out cloudy due to the frozen carbon dioxide sediment, trapped in the air in small quantities. After being processed through a paper filter, liquid air becomes transparent."

Poor girl! She can't have much fun in this godforsaken place. Did she and her father really volunteer to this exile? I thought.

"When liquid air evaporates, the process begins with the boiling of nitrogen, whose boiling point is minus one hundred ninety-four degrees Celsius, then argon. What else is produced during liquid air evaporation?" she suddenly asked, catching my absentminded gaze.

"Argon," I replied mechanically, having caught the last sentence delivered in her lovely voice. Eleonora frowned.

"You are not listening," she said reproachfully.

"Forgive me, but I'd fallen out of the sky only a few hours ago. You must agree going from such an unusual journey to a lecture about liquid air..."

The face of my stern teacher became lit by a smile. Suddenly, unable to resist, she burst out laughing like a child.

"You are right, you need to rest and recover."

I was very glad of this change and asked her, "Tell me how I managed to survive?"

"Someone noticed you. The fans were stopped and you landed fairly softly onto the first grate. The tube has an entire set of sieves for catching various deposits. You'll see them when you examine it. Tomorrow is Sunday, I'll show you."

"Another question..."

But Eleonora was once again absorbed in her work.

"Go rest," she said with gentle imperiousness.

My face must have betrayed disappointment because, having glanced at me, the girl added with her usual kindly smile, "Why don't we meet later today, at the library, after six. Second level, number forty-one." She nodded and returned to her work.

I went back to my room.

VI.   THE UNDERGROUND CITY

On the second day of my "imprisonment", I became pretty well-acquainted with the underground settlement, Eleonora always happy to explain.

The first level was designated for living quarters and offices. Technical experts were housed here, Mr. Bailey himself, The Engelbrechts, engineers, and officers.

"Officers?" I asked with some surprise. Eleonora was taken aback. Apparently, she realized she told me more than she should have and wasn't certain how to correct her mistake.

"Such a large settlement can't be left without protection," she replied. "We have a kind of police or guard squad. Its overseen by several people we call officers. Please don't tell anyone what I told you. Mr. Bailey asked me not to tell you about our guards, and I blurted it out…. Like a stupid girl!" she said, angry with herself.

I assured the girl I would keep mum.

"How big is your police?" I asked. But Eleonora told me she knew nothing else about the city's armed forces.

"The levels are numbered from top to bottom," she continued to familiarize me with the unusual arrangement. "The medium-level specialists live in the two outward hallways of the second level."

I too lived in the second level and asked, jokingly offended," Like me?"

"Yes, like you," Eleonora replied. "Except they know more than you. Libraries and laboratories are located along the inner corridor. The third level is for workers. It also houses food stores, kitchens, dining halls, baths, clubs, and the cinema."

"Even cinema!"

"Yes, cinema and theater. What's so surprising? If we didn't have any entertainment, many of us would have died of boredom."

"Isn't it easier to get out if you are bored?" Eleonora seemed not to hear my question."

"The fourth level or the first under ground is taken up by the machines that extract nitrogen from liquid air and transform it into ammonia, nitric acid, and cyanimide – a substance essential in industry and agriculture." She spoke without pausing, as if afraid I might interrupt her again. "We produce over a million tons of nitric acid a year and keep expanding production. In addition, we produce oxygen. One of the sectors in the fourth level is designated for sorting materials coming from the outside through the main tube. There is an entire system of sieves in the tube, starting from those big enough for a person to crawl through and ending with the ones so fine they stop even dust.

"Were Nikola and I 'sorted' out there?"

"Yes. The most unexpected objects and creatures sometimes end up in the tube. Mostly, the tube sucks in broken trees. Sometimes, the wind brings in enormous uprooted cedars, firs, pines, and larches. All this material is used for heating. In spring and fall, the tube sucks in countless birds. We freeze some of them as part of our annual provision preparation. The rest are cooled with liquid air, turned into fragile stone, and ground into powder to be stored away or, perhaps, exported. Sometimes small predators end up in the tube, or even larger ones – Arctic wolves, foxes. A few times we were visited, after an aerial journey, by bears, and even tigers! In the fifth level, there's a tube that discards the unusable trash. The air in all the underground levels – from fourth to eight – is

39

converted to liquid air. There is a storage space at every level. The most storage is in the sixth level. The seventh and eighth level are the most interesting ones. In the seventh level we use liquid air to obtain liquid hydrogen at the temperature only twenty degrees above absolute zero. We use liquid hydrogen to liquefy helium. That is the hardest, most complex part of our operation. The entire eighth level is dedicated to liquid helium – our most valuable product. We already have several hundred thousand liters."

"But what is the purpose of this gigantic operation?"

"We don't ask about Mr. Bailey's commercial affairs," Eleonora replied, repeating the words I heard from her father.

I wanted to ask a few more questions – where the engine room was, what was in the underground caves? But the bell rang summoning us to breakfast, and I didn't get to find out anything else.

That was on Sunday, when Eleonora and I walked along the "avenue" in the first level – a long circular corridor. The endless walking in circles was dull. As I looked at the numbered doors, I thought I was in an enormous prison. The impression was exacerbated by the fact the corridor was entirely empty. It was as if the "prisoners" weren't allowed out.

I discovered later the inhabitants of the underground city, especially those living in the privileged first level, had the opportunity to go for walks in the surrounding mountains and woods. And, of course, there wasn't a single person who didn't prefer walks outside in the fresh air, to the endless circling along the "prison" corridor.

When the bell rang, doors started opening, people came out, and the corridor came to live. I watched the dwellers of the settlement with great interest. There were no women. It was truly a male city, and Eleonora was, apparently, the same kind of exception as a captain's daughter on a sail ship. They were all young. The eldest couldn't have been more than thirty-five years of age.

I searched in vain for people in military uniforms among them. The "officers" weren't there; everyone wore civilian clothes. However, the particular crispness of movement suggested some of them had served in the military. One could unmistakably tell which ones had been through the service.

I was a newcomer and a stranger among them. Like all courteous people, they didn't stare at me. They greeted my companion politely, gave me a brief glance, and kept going, chatting merrily in, alas, a strange language.

People living in the first level had their own dining hall. I very much wanted to get in there to have a chance to become closer acquainted with the local "aristocracy". But Mr. Bailey took measures to limit my interactions with others. I was kept at the laboratory until workers returned to their room; I was expected to arrive to work later – after everyone had already gone. Besides, I had no access to the communal dining hall. My dinner was served at my room, and I had breakfast at the lab with Eleonora. On Sundays, my breakfast was also delivered to my room.

I said good bye to Eleonora and took an elevator to the second level.

I wanted so much to see the workers, I decided to try a small violation of the rules set for me. Without going to my room, I took the elevator to the third level, and walked down the hallway toward the crowd headed toward the dining hall. The nature of this crowd struck me deeply. I knew I was seeing the working population of the settlement, still, they weren't anything like the workers I expected to see in any place with a rigid class system.

This crowd looked no different than the one living upstairs. They had the same elegant, well-made clothes, the same elegant manners, the same proportionate build, well-trained, healthy, agile rather than muscular bodies, and faces of true intellectuals. The difference between the dwellers of the first and third levels became noticeable only if one observed very closely. It wasn't even a difference but a slight trait existing, for example, within the same society class, but in the different circles, such as *nouveau riche* capitalists and "old money".

Just like in the first level, there were no women or elderly. The crowd was exclusively young and male.

I was surprised and intrigued by these peculiarities. But couldn't stay longer to continue my observations. I rushed back to the second level. In my room, I found William who gave me a suspicious look; I explained to him I accidentally went down an extra level.

I turned my attention to my breakfast, watching William surreptitiously. Of course, he was appointed to spy on me. But that wasn't what interested me most at the moment. I watched his face and compared him to those I saw in the corridors. He was somewhat older than the others, but he looked just as healthy and well-groomed. A director of a large factory could have a face like that. Yet, here he was, serving me breakfast like a valet!

Strange city and Mr. Bailey's strange factory...

VII.   AN UNSUCCESSFUL ESCAPE

The work at the lab continued. A few days later, I even managed to earn Eleonora's praise.

"You're getting there," she noted.

At a different time and under different circumstances, this praise would have pleased me tremendously. But I wasn't planning to make my career here and end my life as one of Mr. Bailey's uncomplaining employees. I kept thinking how to escape. When I returned to my Spartan cell after work, I waited for Nikola who returned a little later, and we got to planning in whispers.

Nikola had been appointed to work with other Yakuts in the tube used to get rid of the trash from the main tube and from the rest of the settlement. Air pressure threw all of it into an enormous abyss outside of the crater. Nikola, who managed to introduce himself to the Chinese cooks, and somehow communicate with them, told me about certain utilities of our city.

Nothing was wasted. I already knew about the game ending up in the tube. More fresh meat was obtained by hunting. The settlement's dwellers hunted, armed with compressed air rifles. There was another interesting hunting method – large pray was attacked by using bombs filled with liquid air enclosed in insulated shells.

One only had to turn a switch to start a heat reaction inside each bomb. Liquid air expanded, turning into a gas, and a bomb tore an animal apart with the same force as dynamite.

Nikola explained to me only the functional side of this weapon, but I could figure out its design. Liquid air wasn't the only source of energy used at the settlement. Another source of energy unknown to me drove all of the super-powerful machines of this unusual factory. When I asked Eleonora for explanation, she replied, "That is not my area."

There are too many industrial secrets at this factory, I thought. It's not enough for Bailey to deprive me of my freedom and turn me into his slave – what if he is forcing me to work in the interests of foreign military? What if all this liquid air will turn into a terrible weapon in their hands? No, I have to get away to warn the government of danger through the nearest office.

Several times, I had Nikola explain to me how the tube was set up in great detail – the plan on the wall provided only a basic schematic. Nikola explained. The tube was at least two kilometers long. At one point, it opened at the very edge of the chasm, but, gradually, the garbage built up under the tube until it created a kind of landing half a kilometer wide. It was big enough to build rails for wagonettes to take the stuff over to the chasm. There was a fairly steep slope at the edge of the landing. The chasm's walls were even steeper, but in Nikola's opinion, it was possible to climb out of it. That was our only path to escape.

I walked over to the plan once again and carefully examined the drawing of the tube. Suddenly, I noticed at some symbols – there were arrows scratched around the end of the tube, with exclamations marks over them.

What did this mean? Who put these marks there? Was it my predecessor, who used to live in this room – another captive like me – trying to warn me not to go that way because there was some danger? The arrows could mean wind direction. But the wind was blowing out of the tube to carry out the garbage. The outside air was pulled in through the central tube in the crater. According to Nikola, there was no wind at all in the side tube during garbage removal and at night, when people slept. In any case, we had no other choice. I could not delay when I knew I had to warn the authorities.

Without further ado, Nikola and I decided to set out the next night, as soon as everyone was asleep.

Are there guards on duty? I wondered. It would be difficult to avoid them, since the lights in the corridors stayed on twenty-four hours – I knew as much. Besides, it was risky to go anywhere in our fairly light indoor clothes. Fall was starting and, despite the warmer temperatures, there could be freezing spells at night. Winter came very quickly in these parts. I was a little less concerned about food. While we were unarmed, Nikola would be with me – he knew how to make bow and arrows, and even rope traps from his own hair. He knew thousands of ways to capture birds, animals, and birds, and we were in no danger of starving to death.

We sat quietly in our room, listening to the distant sounds. Engines hummed somewhere deep underground, and wind howled in the tube above us. Soon, this sound subsided too – the labs sere closed at night.

At midnight, I nodded to Nikola, and we were on our way. Nikola walked ahead of me. We passed through the entire corridor without any trouble or meeting anyone, took an elevator to the fifth level, climbed up a small ladder, and ended up in a tiny space – no bigger than an elevator – with a door leading into the side tube. The room was occupied by a sleeping guard. I staggered back, but Nikola spoke to him quickly and quietly in Yakut language. I recognized Ivan the Senior. Nikola was clearly trying to convince Ivan of something, while the latter shook his head, sighed, and scratched his thin little beard.

"Won't let us in," Nikola explain. "Very scared, says we shouldn't. Scared to die."

Turning to Ivan, Nikola once again tried convincing him to let us through. Ivan hesitated. Finally, he gave up, opened the door leading into the tube, and stepped over the threshold.

"He'll go with us," Nikola explained.

The tube was as big as a railroad tunnel. When the door closed behind us, we found ourselves in complete darkness. No matter how quietly we tried to walk, our footsteps echoed in the tube lined with metal sheets. The tube turned gently toward the end. When we rounded the turn, I suddenly saw the pale light of the moon. I was moved by it – it was a symbol of freedom. A few more steps, and we would be out of our prison! I could smell rotten leaves and moss.

The opening grew wider. The moonlight fell onto the walls of the tube. Closer to the end, I saw metal bars crossing the tube like a small bridge. Nikola was just about to put his foot on this bridge, but I tugged on his sleeve and stopped. I wondered whether this bridge was set up to trigger an alarm. The bridge wasn't very wide, but it was hard to jump over it. I got to thinking how we might get around this obstacle. Nikola didn't understand me and urged me to keep going. I explained my concerns to him.

We discussed our options. Nikola proposed a plan: he and I would lift up Ivan and throw him across the bridge, since he was the smallest and lightest of us. Then Ivan would bring some boards or branches, and we would build a "bridge over a bridge" to get across without having to touch the metal bars. Ivan didn't like the idea of this small aerial trip – he was afraid of getting hurt.

"I can run," he replied. "Sideways, sideways..."

Before we had a chance to object, Ivan stepped back, took a running start, and dashed across the round wall of the tube to the side from the bridge. He made the first few steps, slipped on the smooth, damp slope, and crashed onto the metal bridge. If the bridge was connected with any sort of alarm system, it was bound to trigger it!

We had no choice but to ignore the bridge and run after Ivan. I was out of the tube in two leaps, Nikola following. We ran down the rails, dodging the wagonettes. In two or three minutes, we ran half of the distance between us and the slope. I wasn't afraid of falling into a soft trash heap.

I ran as fast as I could; bandy-legged Nikola was keeping up, but Ivan, who hadn't done any running in a long time, was lagging behind. I slowed down to wait for him, but Nikola shouted, as he passed me, "He'll catch up! Run!" and surged forward.

I sped up after Nikola. We could see the edge of the landing. Gloomy rocks lit by the moon rose on the other side of the chasm.

Suddenly, I heard a sound behind me. The sound strengthened and became an even, powerful hum. At the same time, I felt a head wind. I was running evenly, and the wind had nothing to do with my speed. Perhaps, it's the central fan? It was too early. Work started at six in the morning, and it couldn't have been later than one.

The sound rose in pitch, and the headwind became so powerful I had to lean forward. My run slowed down. I was gasping. The air grew denser. I understood – a fan has been turned on behind us. I didn't know the outlet tube could not only blow the air out but also suck it in.

So that's the meaning of the arrows and exclamation marks on the plan! A thought flickered through my mind. At the same moment, the wind howled like an enraged beast seeing its prey slipping out of its clutches.

The wind became a hurricane. I leaned forward even further and tried to push through this invisible "wall" of air pushing harder and harder against me. But I couldn't make another step. Nikola fell to the ground and crawled. I followed his example, but it didn't help. We made incredible effort clutching at the ground with our hands and feet, but the wind dislodged us and pulled us back.

Our lungs were filled with air like balloons and ready to burst. I was dizzy, my temples were pounding. We were exhausted but refused to give up. Our hands and feet were bleeding. If only we could make it to the edge of the landing. But we could no longer see it. The wind turned my head back, and I saw Ivan. His body twirled, bounced, and flew toward the tube's opening like a tumble weed.

Something soft hit against my head, but I couldn't turn it to see what it was. I could only guess it was Nikola. I started losing consciousness from suffocation. All our struggle was in vain. My muscles grew week, my arms surrendered to the air current. I was carried back into the tube where I finally passed out.

VIII.   "MISTER FATUM"

I came to in the same tube, not far from the door. Nikola and Ivan were sprawled next to me. This time, I was almost completely unscathed. Apparently, the fan slowed down as soon as we flew back into the tube, and the compressed air slowed us down. I shook Nikola by the shoulder, he sighed and said, as if delirious, "Very, very windy."

Shortly, Ivan showed signs of life too.

We went back through the door. Ivan shook his head, said good bye to us, and resumed his post, while we returned to our room. The entire underground city was still asleep. We reached our room having met no one at all. I fell into my bed in desperation, not bothering to undress, expecting someone to come in at any moment and arrest us for our attempted escape.

Didn't anyone notice us? The fan may have been activated automatically, and everyone here is so used to humming noises, they probably don't even notice, a comforting thought popped into my mind. I fell asleep.

The bell woke us up at the usual time – six in the morning. Nikola had to leave before me. I lay in bed with my eyes closed and heard him getting dressed, huffing, and humming a song. I envied his placidity. I fell asleep again until the second bell at seven-thirty. I quickly downed a glass of coffee with crackers and went to the lab.

"You look pale today," Eleonora said after taking one look at me.

"I slept badly," I replied.

"Why is that?"

"Thoughts. I can't reconcile myself with my captivity and I never will."

49

Eleonora frowned. I interpreted the expression my own way. Maybe she liked me and was disappointed I preferred freedom to her company? But, apparently, she was thinking about something else entirely.

"One must learn to obey the inevitable," she said sadly as if she was in the same position as I. I was surprised and intrigued.

"Inevitable? Mr. Bailey, an entrepreneur running rather questionable operations, a foreigner who illegally set up shop in our territory doesn't appear to be anything like *fatum*[1], to be followed and obeyed. If you are such a fatalist..." I began with some irritation.

"I am not a fatalist," she replied. "But one need not be a fatalist to understand a simple fact that circumstances are sometimes stronger than we are."

"Or rather, we are weaker than the circumstances." I refused to give up, sensing I had stumbled onto a painful topic.

"Ah, you just don't understand!" she replied and returned to her work.

But I didn't want to miss my chance. The girl was clearly in the kind of mood when, with some persistence on my part, she might have told me something she wouldn't have at any other time.

"Explain to me then!" I replied. "The only thing I've understood so far is you are a prisoner here, just like me."

"You are mistaken," the girl replied. "Just this morning, my father tried convincing me to leave here and... Mr. Bailey did not object..."

---

[1] In Roman mythology – the will of the gods.

"Nevertheless, you don't leave. Something is keeping you. This means you are indeed a prisoner – if not of Mr. Bailey, then, of the circumstances that do not allow you to leave. Wait, I think I know! You said your father was convincing you to leave. With him or without him?"

Eleonora was taken aback.

"Without," she replied quietly.

"Then it's clear. You don't want to leave without him, and he either cannot leave or does not want to. Or rather, Mister Fatum is not letting him go."

Eleonora smiled with her eyes only and said nothing.

"You told me once," I continued, encouraged, "your family is very well-known in Sweden, although not in the sense suggested by your name. You said your ancestor was Engelbrecht, the miner, who led the 15th century rebellion against King Eric of Pomerania[2]. An honorable ancestor! Can it be that over the last five-hundred years the Engelbrechts have lost the entire legacy of the famous miner and are now only capable of bowing before their oppressors?"

The blow turned out to be too strong. I didn't expect to cause Eleonora so much pain. She had told me about her rebellious ancestor many times and was clearly proud of him. This disadvantageous comparison both moved and angered her. Eleonora suddenly rose, straightened her shoulders, and tipped her head back. Her cheeks turned pale, her brows drew together. Her eyes flashed in a way I'd never seen before. She

---

[2] Engelbrecht (Engelbrechtson) defeated King Eric of Denmark, Sweden, and Norway (dethroned in 1436), and the lower classes' candidate to be a new ruler. However, the aristocracy managed to come up with a candidate of their own and set him onto the throne. Several years later, Engelbrecht was assassinated.

looked at me angrily and said in a halting voice, "You... you..." Her breath caught. "You don't understand anything," she finished quietly and suddenly covered her face and started crying.

I was at a complete loss. I had no intention of upsetting her so. I only wanted her to be honest with me. Her anger saddened me.

"I am sorry," I said in a voice so pitiful it would have melted a rock (and Eleonora's heart was not a rock).

Her shoulders stopped shaking, and she quickly regained control over herself.

"Please, forgive me, I didn't mean to offend you."

Eleonora pulled her hands away from her face and forced a smile.

"Let's forget this. My nerves are a bit on edge. Careful!" she suddenly exclaimed, noticing I dropped a piece of metal on the table, next to a cube of solid alcohol that looked like glass (we had just finished freezing pure alcohol using liquid air). "Don't you know solid alcohol doesn't burn but explodes from an impact?"

"Ether freezes into a crystalline mass," I continued jokingly, imitating her mentoring tone. "In contact with liquid air a rubber tube turns hard and fragile, and can be broken into pieces or ground into powder; live flowers look like porcelain, and a wool hat can be shattered into pieces."

"You forgot to mention properties of metals in contact with liquid air," Eleonora said, with a sincere smile this time.

I continued, "Lead's resistance to rupture increases nearly twofold," I replied. "Elasticity and tensile strength increase for most metals."

"That's enough," she interrupted. "Let's get back to work."

She picked up a glass with amalgamated sides, looked at the sky-blue liquid inside and, noticing a speck of dust on the surface, suddenly lowered one finger into it.

"What are you doing?!" It was my turn to shout, because I was extremely alarmed. "You'll freeze your finger off!"

I'd only recently watched her "demonstration", in which a kettle filled with liquid air and set on top of a piece of ice started "boiling" because even ice was too hot compared to the temperature of liquid air. Such low temperature would cause more damage to the body than white-hot metal.

Much to my surprise, Eleonora didn't scream or pull her finger out of the glass. She shook it off and showed to me. The finger was unharmed.

"Liquid air immediately adjacent to the finger evaporates quickly, because its temperature is so much lower. It forms a kind of shell made of liquid air vapors – see? – which briefly protects the finger from any damage. Don't even think about it," she said, noticing I too reached for the glass. "One must do this skillfully, quickly, and without touching the walls of the vessel."

We became absorbed in work. Eleonora seemed to have forgotten about our argument, but I could not. Poor Nora! I dared to call her that in my mind. Apparently she too was one of Bailey's unfortunate victims. This discovery increased my growing affection for the girl. At the same time, my memory filed away another crime committed by Mr. Bailey.

Without realizing it, I started thinking of how to escape with Eleonora.

The lab was quiet. We worked away diligently. Suddenly, I was startled by a sound similar to a gun-shot.

"You put the stopper in too deep again!" Nora reproached me.

Yes, it was my fault. Liquid air evaporated quickly at room temperature and pushed out the stoppers by sheer pressure.

"If I put the stopper too deep – it explodes, if not deep enough – it evaporates too fast," I grumbled jokingly.

"You find that difficult? At least you can't complain about our working condition," Nora replied. "We have plenty of fresh air."

"Is that why your cheeks are so pink?" Nora cast a mischievous feminine look at me for the first time, which encouraged me tremendously – this meant she wasn't angry!

The door opened, William came in and said something in English. Nora translated.

"Mr. Bailey wants to see Mr. Klimenko. Time for punishment," she added with a smile.

Does everyone know about our attempted escape? I wondered. This made me anxious, but I was encouraged by Nora's calm smile. Alas, I didn't know Mr. Bailey only ever asked to see anyone in person "for punishment". Nora's father was an exception. In the underground settlement, he was the highest court with no right of appeal.

I set out with a heavy heart.

"I hope it's not too bad!" Nora shouted after me.

IX.   "THE ROYAL PARDON"

Nikola and Ivan were already in Mr. Bailey's office, accompanied by two guards armed by automatic pistols powered by compressed air. Mr. Bailey was standing by his desk.

"Come in!" he said to me sternly without offering me a seat.

I walked over to his desk. Mr. Bailey sat down. I didn't want to stand in front of him and also sat down. Bailey flashed his eyes at me. His eyebrows moved.

"Did you try to escape?" he asked me, although it sounded more like a statement than a question.

"We went for a walk," I said with a smile.

"Don't lie and don't deny anything! You tried to escape. I have warned you of the consequences."

Mr. Bailey gave an order to one of the armed guards. He walked up to me and invited me to follow him.

The trial continued less than a minute – apparently, all that was left was to carry out the sentence. I rose and followed him. Two others escorted Nikola and Ivan. At the corner, Ivan and Nikola were taken one way and I – the other. We went downstairs and followed the corridor. The guard stopped by a narrow metal door, opened it, and rather unceremoniously pushed me into a small cell with solid, smooth, metal walls and a small electric lamp on the ceiling. The door slammed shut, the lock clicked. I was left alone.

Solitary confinement. It's not so bad. I have it easy, I thought, examining my prison. It was dry and clean, but cold. A Celsius thermometer hung on the wall. Such thermometers were in every room and even in the corridors of the underground city – everyone kept a very close eye on the temperature. The thermometer read only six degrees above zero.

After all the tribulations of the sleepless night, I felt weak and shattered. I was sleepy. My legs barely held me up. But there wasn't even a chair in the room. I settled down on the cold, stone floor and dosed off. However, I soon woke up from cold. I felt a shiver. I rose and looked up at the thermometer. It showed minus two. *What does it mean?* I thought. *A mechanic's oversight or intentional?*

To keep warm, I started pacing around the cell, but it was so small, I could only make two steps forward and two steps back. I started jumping and swinging my arms. I grew even more tired, but managed to improve my circulation. However, the moment I sat down, cold wrapped itself around me with renewed strength. My teeth chattered. I once again looked at the thermometer and saw minus eleven.

I felt the cold seeping into me, chilling my back, and clenching around my heart. But it wasn't just from the low temperature. A terrible thought occurred to me – Mr. Bailey was trying to freeze me to death! Blinded by instinct, I ran up to the door and started knocking.

"Open up! Open up!" I screamed frantically. But no one responded. A pounded until my hands bled and finally slid onto the floor.

"Circumstances can be stronger than we are. One need not be a fatalist to understand this." I remembered Eleonora's words. Still, at least I fought, I tried to escape, and I didn't die without a fight! And she... Although, perhaps she fought too—I remembered Nikola's story about the corpse tied to the ship's railing. That was how Mr. Bailey dealt with his enemies. Perhaps, Eleonora was right, and it was hopeless to resist Bailey.

It was so cold! My arms and legs ached unbearably. I rubbed my fingers, but they stiffened and no longer flexed. I rose with difficulty and looked at the thermometer. Twenty below zero. My struggle was over! I surrendered to my fate.

At some point, I passed out sitting on the floor. After all, death by freezing wasn't all that terrible. It was better than death in an electric chair. Soon, I would feel no pain and simply fall asleep.

There was rustling by the door. Or did I imagine it? I tried to get up but cold restricted my movements. All was quiet. I must have imagined the sound.

The cell seemed to grow warmer. But it had to be an illusion. Human body radiated heat into the air, decreasing the temperature difference between the body and the surrounding air, creating an illusion of cold. This meant the end was near. Time passed, but I remained conscious, and the sensation of warmth increased. Odd! I have never frozen to death before, but was certain that's not what it felt like. To check my senses, I tried moving my fingers and, to my surprise, realized they moved easily, even though a short time before I couldn't even bend them. I looked at the thermometer.

Plus five!

The temperature was going up! I was saved, and my fears were in vain. Apparently, Mr. Bailey merely wished to scare me.

A few minutes later, the temperature rose to plus twelve, which was normal for the living quarters of the underground city. I rose and tried stretching my limbs. My fingers turned red and swollen. But I felt my blood warming them quickly. Since the temperature rose as evenly as it dropped I avoided frostbite.

What was to happen to me next? How long would I be held in solitary confinement?

As if to answer my questions, something once again rustled behind the door, and I heard the sound of a key being turned. The door opened, William came in and gestured for me to follow him.

I no longer doubted I was to be kept alive and cheerfully strolled out of the cell. William once again took me to Mr. Bailey's study.

This time, Bailey invited me to sit, rose from behind his desk, and started pacing around the study.

"Mr. Klimenko," he said. "You have earned the death sentence and ought to thank Ms. Engelbrecht for being kept alive."

I looked at Bailey in surprise, "I sentenced you to death. I chose for you the easiest way for transitioning to the underworld. I had already given the order to carry out the sentence. But we have a shortage of qualified workers. Miss Eleonora can't manage by herself. You were her assistant and, before dealing with you, I decided to ask whether you provided significant help in her work. She did not know you were in danger. I simply asked her to provide some feedback. She said you were an excellent worker and an irreplaceable assistant. She resisted when I suggested I might... transfer you to another job. And I had to... cancel my decision. You have been pardoned!" he concluded solemnly, apparently expecting gratitude on my part.

But I said nothing and only nodded. Mr. Bailey smiled crookedly.

"Ms. Engelbrecht warmly... even very warmly described your contributions. She knew nothing of your attempted escape. Unless you told her something?"

"I said nothing," I replied.

"You are ungrateful! You tried to run away... from her!"

"I tried to run away from captivity," I corrected Mr. Bailey.

"And she – her presence – did not dissuade you?"

"I ask you not to meddle in my personal feelings and relationships, Mr. Bailey," I said dryly. "They are none of your business."

"You think so?" he asked. "No, Mr. Klimenko, they are very much my business!"

I understood Mr. Bailey's implications. Apparently, he wished to know whether we have fallen in love, Eleonora and I. Love would have made Eleonora's life easier and tied me to the underground settlement better than any chain. I was so outraged by his conniving, my budding feelings toward Eleonora were in grave danger. Bailey was a poor psychologist. He clearly didn't know nothing could undermine love more than being forced into it. He didn't even try his willingness to play matchmaker in order to turn marital ties into chains holding me to his "factory".

"Remember," Bailey continued, "I demanded from you a promise not to run from here, but did not insist you give that promise. I don't believe in people's honestly. I particularly don't believe... don't be so nervous! – don't believe the word of a man given under the circumstances in which you find yourself. As your Russian proverb says, no matter how much you feed a wolf, he always looks toward the forest. I decided you should experience for yourself it is impossible to run away from here.

Then you'll settle down and work. And you have done so. Now you are one of us. I think you won't be too bored, unless you have a heart of stone."

I rose from my seat. I must have looked very sinister, because Mr. Bailey stepped away from me and laughed dryly.

"Come, don't be angry," he said more peaceably. "I said nothing offensive to you or to Miss Eleonora. She is a beautiful girl, and any man would have been honored to have her. Come with me. I can show you much you haven't seen yet. This will be of some use to you."

X.   AN UNDERGROUND JOURNEY

Mr. Bailey opened a secret door and walked into the next room. I followed him.

"Incidentally," Mr. Bailey said, "if you are interested, you may listen to the latest radio reports. Your death is already being mourned. You and Nikola drowned in the Lena. All that was left was a bag with instruments. It was very cleanly done, Mister Dead Man."

As he said that, Bailey walked up to a large case and opened it. In it hung several suits resembling those for deep sea diving. Mr. Bailey corrected my mistake, "These are not for diving. These suits can be used to walk among stars, at temperatures barely above absolute zero. They are made of a completely non-conductive material and come with oxygen canisters."

"What is this for?" I asked, pointed at a metal spike with a round tip attached to the helmet.

"It's an antenna. The suits are equipped with their own tiny radios. We will use them to communicate. Get dressed!"

I took one suit off the hanger. It was lighter than a diving suit. Mr. Bailey helped me get dressed and carefully buttoned the suit with special buttons.

"We are ready," he said. I heard him fine even though our heads were enclosed within thick helmets. "Convenient, isn't it? This could have been priceless for deep sea divers."

"Of course, you didn't bother to offer this invention to society," I noted somewhat acidly.

"Society!" he replied with disdain. "What can society give me in exchange? I have no time for such nonsense."

Mr. Bailey walked to a wall, turned a lever, and a trap door opened in the middle of the floor. I looked down and saw a small ladder leading down to a landing surrounded by a light metal railing.

"Go ahead," Bailey invited me.

I climbed down to the landing, Bailey followed me, turned a lever on the railing, and we smoothly slid down. Our descent continued for some time. When the elevator stopped, Bailey opened the doors, and we stepped out. Directly in front of us was a low iron door. Bailey opened it, and we found ourselves in a small, very narrow room. Bailey opened the second door – I couldn't tell what it was made of – it was black and smooth, like ebony.

"It's made of a substance that does not conduct heat," Bailey explained.

There was another small room, and another door. We passed through five such rooms and opened five doors.

"In each chamber, the temperature is approximately fifty degrees Celsius lower than in the previous one," Bailey continued explaining. "We are about to enter a place, where temperature approaches that of interstellar space."

Mr. Bailey opened the sixth door, and I saw an astonishing sight!

Before us was an enormous underground cavern. Dozens of lamps lit a large lake, its water an uncommonly pretty blue color. It was as if a piece of blue sky somehow fell into this cave.

"Liquid air," Bailey said. I was stunned. Until then, I only saw liquid air in small vessels at the lab. I could have never imagined it was possible to liquefy and preserve such an enormous quantity of air.

At the same time, I felt my suit shrinking and I couldn't understand why.

"The pressure is very high here. We would have been crushed, had it not been for particularly high elasticity of the cloth our suits are made of. With Mr. Engelbrecht's help, I was able to make certain liquid air almost didn't evaporate. Notice the ceiling. It's tiled with heat-resistant material. Even lamps in this cave are different – they are made of luminescent bacteria! Absolutely cold light. Yes, this blue lake would have been sufficient to bring life to the Moon – to give it an atmosphere, if only the Moon could hold onto it. I have several such lakes. But it's not enough, not enough by far. Liquid air density is only eight hundred times higher than that of the atmosphere. We would need entire oceans to liquefy the entire atmosphere. Calculate for yourself: the area of the globe is approximately five hundred ten million square kilometers. Which means, the air layer just one kilometer above Earth's surface has the volume of at least half-billion cubic kilometers. The air of more or less homogenous density stretches at least eight kilometers up. That's over five trillion kilograms, or one millionth of Earth's mass. So much unused raw material!"

"Raw material?" I blurted out despite myself. Bailey continued, unperturbed, "Of course, it's very difficult to calculate the exact amounts of air. The interplanetary space transitions into Earth's atmosphere gradually, through a zone of dissipated gases. The exact chemical composition of air has been determined as high as nine kilometers. Balloons with recording devices rise a little higher than thirty-seven and a half kilometers. Passing meteorites catch fire as high as one hundred fifty to two-hundred kilometers. This means, even at that altitude, the air is fairly dense. Nissel noticed the burning of meteors at the altitude of seven hundred eighty kilometers. The same is indicated by the Aurora borealis. People have admired this celestial light display, but only recently discovered the spectrum of these uncommonly lovely lights consists primarily of inert gases, primarily helium. Oxygen, nitrogen, neon, and helium spectral lines show up in the northern lights at the altitude of eight hundred kilometers. It's possible; the electrical forces whirl, pull away, and lift to the upper layers of the atmosphere the individual atoms of the gases comprising it. In any case, these atoms continue to exist even at this tremendous altitude. But that is not all. You mustn't think the atmosphere exists only above Earth's surface. American scientist Clerk calculated gaseous substances comprise three hundredth of the mass of Earth's crust as deep as sixteen kilometers. So, the total amount of air..."

"You aren't planning to strip the entire globe of its atmosphere, are you?" I exclaimed in astonishment.

"Why not?" Mr. Bailey replied. "Come along, you'll see it's quite possible. Svante Engelbrecht is a genius. He is worth the money I pay him."

Is it really all about the money?! I thought. Perhaps, Nora's father is a greedy man. Being paid a lot of money, he buried himself in this burrow along with his daughter and has no wish to return home. His daughter is wasting away from boredom, but doesn't wish to leave her father. Is that what Nora's drama all about?

"Earth without its atmosphere – what a terrible catastrophe that would be!"

"Oh yes," Bailey replied sarcastically. "People will start suffocating, plants will die too, icy cold shall descend on Earth from the stars. Life will stop, and the globe will become as dead as the frozen Moon. And so it shall be!" Bailey exclaimed.

At that moment I felt I was dealing with a madman.

"You wish to destroy humanity?" I asked.

"I simply don't care about humanity. It's headed for destruction on its own. After all, our planet won't be here forever. I wasn't the one who doomed it to die. What difference does it make whether it happens sooner or later?"

"It makes a great difference. Humankind could live millions of years. Our Earth is very young – much younger than Mars."

"Can you guarantee mankind will live millions of years? One wayward comet would be sufficient to bring your Earth to its untimely death."

"Chances of that are negligible."

"From your nearsighted standpoint of an earthworm. Astronomers say otherwise. They have observed large flashes of light in all corners of the Universe. If we consider the cosmic scale in our galaxy, this backward alley of the Universe called the Milky Way, collisions take place as often as car crashes in the streets of a large city."

"Yes, but for us Earthworms, the intervals between these catastrophes equal millions of years. What is your purpose in trying to destroy humankind?"

"I told you I didn't care for it. I don't wish to destroy it, but I also don't wish to give up my goals for the sake of saving it."

"What goals?"

Mr. Bailey did not reply.

We walked along the stunning blue lake. Barely noticeable mist rose above it. Despite all precaution, liquid air was still evaporating a little. The warmth from Earth's core and sun had its effect even here, through all the layers of insulation.

There was a black door in the wall of the cavern.

"Through here," Mr. Bailey said. He opened the door, we followed a sloping corridor, and entered another cave. It was much smaller. There was no blue lake. It was a store room of some kind. Or rather, an entire store village, with enormous cases of the same black glossy material instead of houses. The "streets" were arranged in a grid, like many American cities. Bailey opened the doors of one case, pulled out a drawer, and showed me its contents – it was filled with shiny balls the size of walnuts. I was interested to hear an explanation.

"You probably know," Bailey began, "a single liter of water at room temperature absorbs up to seven hundred liters of ammonia. At zero degrees Celsius, the amount increases to one thousand forty liters, and the volume of water almost does not increase."

I nodded and replied, "The gas settles in the gaps between water particles."

"Exactly. The gaps between gas molecules are enormous with respect to the size of the molecules themselves. The arrangement of molecules is similar to that of the planets in the solar system – they too are tremendously far apart from each other, compared to their dimensions. If you read Flammarion, you remember what he said about the comets. A comet consisting of thin gases and taking the space of hundreds of thousands cubic kilometers could be fit into a thimble by concentrating these gases. Well then... these are the thimbles. Clever Engelbrecht managed to turn liquid air into an extremely dense substance. This one drawer contains more air than that great lake of liquid air. Try picking up one of the balls!"

I reached out, tried to pick up a ball, but could not do it.

"They are stuck together," I said. Bailey laughed.

"What is the weight of one cubic meter of air at room temperature?" he asked.

"About one kilogram."

"A kilogram and a quarter. This one ball contains one cubic kilometer of air. Even a strong horse might have a tough time moving a cart loaded with one such ball."

I was deeply struck, and Mr. Bailey was clearly very pleased by my astonishment.

"Yes," he repeated, "Engelbrecht is worth the money I pay him. You must see it's not at all impossible to do the same with all of the air. I can imagine the hubbub when people start suffocating!"

Holding out his hand toward the sparkling little spheres, Mr. Bailey said dramatically, "From here, I can rule the world!"

Without knowing it, he repeated the words of Pushkin's *Avaricious Knight* almost verbatim.

"What lies beyond my rule?" I cited out loud and continued,

Like a demon, from now on the world is mine to rule;
My mere wish – and there shall be a palace...
All things obey me, but I'm ruled by nothing;
I am beyond all passions, I am calm;
I know my power – the knowledge is enough...

"Well said," Bailey replied, having listened to me carefully. "I didn't know you were a poet."

"I didn't say it. Pushkin did."

"Doesn't matter. It was well said. Pushkin? I remember. He imitated our Byron and Walter Scott. But I don't like the ending. The mere realization of power is not enough. I am a capitalist, a businessman. Dead capital is like dead weight. I must buy and sell, and so I do. I'm an air merchant! Ha-ha-ha! Who could have thought?"

"Whom do you trade with?" I asked.

"Whom do you think?" Mr. Bailey exclaimed with sudden irritation. "You don't suppose I'll trade with your local purchasing bodies, do you?"

"Do you trade with someone abroad? I can't say it's legal. You have set up shop on our territory."

"Yes, and I process your splendid Russian air and violate the international trade laws, and so on and so forth. I shall trade with Britain, Germany, and France; make a profit, and what then? Are you going to take it away from me? If I go to England, are you going to organize a revolution there to take away my capital?" Mr. Bailey continued with growing irritation. "No, enough! You have ruined the world. There isn't a place on the globe where the Red Menace is not a threat. I could twist you into a pretzel. You have no idea of all my resources. But I am tired of it. I want to calmly and confidently conduct my business."

"Then you might be better off if you moved to the Moon," I said sarcastically.

"That would be very simple! There's nothing funny about it. The Moon is too small to keep an atmosphere, but I could arrange underground dwellings. There would be plenty of air. As for interplanetary travel, I have a few options better than conventional rockets."

"Are you serious?" I asked, looking at him in confusion.

"Completely serious."

"And you'll open a company that will sell air? But didn't you say you were already conducting some trade?"

"I am, and very successfully."

"May I ask with whom?"

"With Mars," he replied. "Yes, with Martians. It's a very profitable market for selling air. Atmospheric pressure on Mars is twelve times lower than ours. Poor Martians don't have enough air. And they pay me very well."

He's mad! I thought. As if it wasn't bad enough!

"Do they come to you or do you send your sales representative to them?"

"What for? I launch these projectiles to Mars from a special canon. Once they get there, they explode and release the air. The Martians use the same method to send me *il*."

"*Il*? What is that?"

"It's a radioactive element capable of producing tremendous energy. This energy powers all my machines, as well as the canon sending the projectiles to Mars. It could also provide the energy for the rocket I'll take to the Moon."

"Why couldn't the Martians come to Earth to get air? Mars is an older planet, and they must be more advanced technologically than we are."

"They are. But they are physically weak. They have been experimenting with space travel for six hundred years. But they always perished, unable to survive in flight. When their bodies became weightless in space, it had a harmful impact on their circulation and other vital functions. The brave travelers invariably died – some on the way, others shortly after returning to Mars. This condition is translated into our language as *levitation*."

"How did you learn all this and establish contact with them?"

Mr. Bailey frowned.

"I told you enough. If you don't believe me, I'll show you *il*. Although, you have already seen me in the swamp when I nearly died picking up one of the Martian packages."

I still didn't believe Bailey – it was all too strange – and continued objecting, "Such a projectile was bound to heat up and turn into gas, like a meteorite, when flying through Earth's atmosphere."

"You said yourself, Martian technology must be far ahead of ours. Their packages are equipped with speed and navigation controls managed remotely by Martian engineers."

I wanted to ask Mr. Bailey a few more questions, but he closed the case and told me, "Let's keep going. I'll show you one more interesting and educational thing."

Bailey brought me to a narrow door, which led into a barely-lit corridor.

"One more question," I said, "why did you set up your factory in Yakutia?"

"Because it's a convenient place for my purposes — the pole of cold."

"But the center Greenland is no warmer – their temperature rarely gets higher than thirty degrees Celsius below zero, even in the summer."

"It's a superficial advantage. As soon as my fans turned on, they would have drawn warmer air from the south and raised Greenland's temperature significantly. In any case, at present, the air temperature is not that important to me. Much less so than in the beginning. Now I have things set up so I could have interstellar cold even at the equator, within the bounds of my underground city of course. Besides, Greenland is swarming with American meteorologists studying the 'motherland of cyclones'. I needed a cozy little corner where no one would interfere with my plans until I had everything set up. Now I have no one to fear, while others have much to fear from me. Anyone who follows the wind will end up in trouble! By the way, I forgot to tell you another bit of news. No one is looking for you any longer, but your expedition still plans to set out as soon as your replacement arrives. I assure you, the entire expedition will die, to the last person! Winter is coming. I'll raise such a storm the expedition members will die before they get to a half point between me and Verkhoyansk."

"The government will send another expedition next summer. They won't leave you alone," I said.

"All the worse for them," Bailey replied and opened the door.

We entered an enormous, round, half-lit cave. Mr. Bailey turned a switch, and bright lights came on. I saw an incredible sight.

Stalactites hung from the ceiling and fancifully shaped stalagmites rose from the ground to meet them. Crystal prisms sparkled all over the ceiling. Spiral columns reminiscent of a Buddhist temple, strange formations on the walls, and lime "curtains" in corners created a surreal effect.

In the middle of the cave, directly across from me, stood an enormous wooly mammoth. Its trunk was outstretched as if this colossus was about to call others to battle. Its enormous legs – each thicker than my torso – were spread, the head – slightly bowed. The mammoth's entire huge body shone as if covered in glass. The mammoth was surrounded by smaller members of the animal kingdom: brown and white bears, wolves, foxes, sables, stoats. It was a veritable ice zoo!

Glossy birds sat on rock ledges – polar owls, geese, ducks, and crows. Along the walls stood the two-legged representatives of the polar and sub-polar regions: Yakuts, Samoyeds, Voguls, Chukchas – all of them in full national costume, armed with home-made bows, arrows, and animal traps. Some looked prepared to shoot, others steered sled dogs or reindeer, yet others were holding harpoons or oars. Next to them were household objects and tools.

It was an entire museum, uncommonly varied and comprehensive. All of the exhibits were covered in a transparent substance that shone like glass and allowed to discern the smallest details.

"Amazing!" I said.

Mr. Bailey chuckled indulgently.

"Your scientists are only planning to set up an ice museum, and I have already done so. You know how permafrost preserves bodies completely intact. That mammoth we dug up has been trapped in permafrost for many thousands of years, but its meat is fresh enough to cook and eat today. Our dogs were very happy to have a few mammoth steaks."

"But you don't just have prehistoric animals here, you also have bears and foxes... Besides, what about these people?"

"Yes, I also collected living samples."

"Living people?"

"Why not? What's the difference? Sooner or later each one of these people would have been mauled by a bear or simply died a natural death and vanished without a trace, as animals do. The fate of those who ended up in my museum is beautiful. The cold preserves them better than embalming kept Egyptian mummies. They are immortal."

"For whom? Who sees them?"

"You, me, does it matter? I have no intention of turning my museum into an educational institution and bequeath it to anyone. It's my whim, my entertainment. You can't have all work and no play! I must have amusement."

"And for that you... killed people?"

"I'm not the first person to say hunting people is the most exciting sport. Although, I don't want you to think I intentionally organized hunting parties to go after the 'two-legged animal'. Not at all! Those here are the ones who were careless enough to wander near my city. No one was supposed to know about it. Those who followed the wind simply never returned."

"But that is not all," he continued after a pause. "I'll show you another exhibit of my museum. Come!"

We continued to an adjacent cave. It was significantly smaller. In the depth of the cave along the walls stood more human statues, gleaming like glass.

We came closer.

"Here, how about this," Mr. Bailey said, pointing at the statues. "This is the fate of anyone who tries to run away from here. You see this pedestal? It was intended for you."

Mr. Bailey turned on the main lamp. Bright light fell upon the statues. I looked closer and shuddered. They were dead and covered in liquid class or some other transparent substance.

"I freeze people and then douse them with water, which instantly turns into ice. They can stay here until the second coming. A very educational sight, no? I show these mummies to the potential escapees after their first attempt, and it has a greatly beneficial effect – the guilty lose all desire to violate the laws I established. Of course, I need workers, especially highly qualified ones."

I counted eleven bodies. Five of them were Yakut, three, apparently Europeans, and the rest looked like Siberian hunters. The thin layer of ice showed them in detail. They wore the clothes they died in. Most faces were calm, only one Yakut had a terrible smile on his face.

"How do you like my 'pantheon'?" Bailey asked.

"It's a revolting sight," I replied. "One must be completely convinced of his invincibility to keep this evidence of crime."

"What, you haven't lost faith in retribution yet?" Bailey asked sarcastically. "Yes, they say one's life is easier with this illusion. But it's time for us to return."

XI. PRISONERS OF THE UNDERGROUND CITY

I returned from our excursion completely exhausted and depressed. And Bailey didn't even show me everything! I didn't see his machine, his deadly weapons, or *il* in action. What I did see was more than enough to leave one unsettled. Bailey turned out to be stronger and more frightening than I could imagine. Fighting him would be extremely difficult. Meanwhile, his insane actions threatened all of humanity.

He remained a puzzle to me. His "commercial" undertakings could not have been solely about profit. Indeed, how would one man placing himself outside of society use boundless riches, especially having doomed all life on Earth to terrible death? Only a maniac would do a thing like that. Perhaps, Bailey had taken to heart the desperation of all tyrants, destined to failure through history and, like Samson decided to perish with his enemies? No. That was insane! People of his class were in no hurry to die as long as they were in good health.

I returned to the lab. Nora saw me and nodded cheerfully. Her fresh face blushed a little. She looked down at a test tube.

"Ms. Engelbrecht," I said rather solemnly, "allow me to thank you."

"For a good review? What nonsense! You are worth it. You are an excellent worker when you don't think too much... And don't cork the beakers with liquid air too tightly... And..."

"It's not nonsense!" I interrupted her warmly. "You saved my life!"

Nora looked at me with surprise and even fear.

"You must be joking."

"Not at all. I was under the penalty of death for attempting to escape."

"Death? I didn't know it was so serious; otherwise I would have tried harder. But who was threatening you? Was it..."

"Of course, it was Mr. Bailey. Oh, he is not at all indulgent to those who doesn't obey his will! Have you ever seen his terrible 'pantheon'?"

Nora shook her head and asked me what I meant. I told her about my excursion through the underground city in Bailey's company and everything I learned from the "air merchant".

To my surprise, Nora listened to me with great interest. Apparently, much of what I told her was news to her. The more I spoke, the more she frowned. Her surprise was replaced with mistrust, her mistrust – with indignation.

Having finished my story, I raised a glass with liquid air and said, "In this glass is a deathly potion for humanity. My life was spared only to assist in the death of others, and the death of our beautiful Earth with all the living creatures on it. I don't know whether to be happy about my escape or drink this?"

The phone rang interrupted my dramatic speech. Nora quickly picked it up.

"Hello... Yes... Mr. Klimenko, Mr. Bailey for you."

I walked over to the phone.

"Yes, it's me... No... Certainly!"

"Is something wrong?" Nora asked when I hung up.

"Mr. Bailey was late. Apparently, he forgot to tell me not to tell you about anything I have seen or heard."

"What did you tell him?"

"I told him I didn't tell you anything and promised not to."

Nora sighed with relief.

She then took from me the glass of liquid air, looked thoughtfully at the blue liquid, and suddenly threw the glass on the floor. The glass broke. The liquid air spilled and started hissing and quickly evaporating on the floor. In a minute, there was nothing left but pieces of glass.

Great! I thought. Now I have an ally!

Nora looked me in the eyes searchingly.

"Did you tell me everything?"

"Everything," I replied and instantly felt awkward: I recalled Mr. Bailey's plans for my marrying Nora. I didn't want to tell her about it. But she noticed my reluctance.

"You are hiding something. You didn't tell me everything!"

"It's nothing; it has nothing to do with our work."

"Don't lie to me. If it was nothing, you wouldn't have been so taken aback."

I was in a difficult predicament and decided to move from defense to offense.

"What about you – do you tell me everything? Remember our conversation, when I upset you with a careless question? Forgive me for bringing it up. You said, 'You don't know anything.' Why didn't you explain to me what I didn't know?"

It was Nora's turn to feel awkward.

"There are things that are difficult to talk about."

"I could use the same argument for my own secrecy."

"No, you cannot. You didn't let me finish. Some things are difficult to talk about. But there are circumstances when silence is no longer an option. And you have to talk about everything, no matter how hard it is."

"Will you tell me?"

"Yes, if you promise not to hide anything from me."

I was hoisted by my own petard. The deal was made, and I had to tell her my secret. I did my best to smooth over Bailey's cynicism.

"Bailey said I had a heart of stone if I decided to run, sacrificing the company of a girl like you for the sake of freedom."

Nora smiled – it sounded like a compliment. But she was smart and soon realized the ulterior motive behind the compliment. She frowned.

"I ought to be grateful to Mr. Bailey for his good opinion," she said. "Unfortunately, Mr. Bailey approaches everything from the commercial standpoint. There was a time when he, himself sought my company. And even then, I knew he was guided by his interests and not his heart. He saw I was bored and missing human society. My father is extremely busy. He loves me very much, but I think he loves science even more," Nora said with some bitterness and jealousy. "My depression interfered with work. And Mr. Bailey — do you understand? He proposed to me."

"And you?" I asked, holding my breath.

"I refused him, of course," Nora replied.

I couldn't hide my sigh of relief.

"I didn't know much about his business at the time and took little interest in it. But I simply didn't like him. For some time, he was hopeful to attract me with his millions, but finally left me alone, when I told him in no uncertain terms, I would leave if he kept pestering me. This frightened him, and he promised to 'forget me'. Apparently, Mr. Bailey had come up with a different version of the same plan, hoping to kill two birds with one stone. Plainly speaking, he wants for the two of us to get married. Doesn't he?"

I blushed. Nora laughed. I felt better. Apparently, this time Mr. Bailey's plans weren't all that unpleasant to her! But Nora instantly cooled me down. Or was it merely feminine trickery? She looked at me mischievously and said in a businesslike manner, "Of course, I have no plans to marry you, Mr. Klimenko."

"Who then?" I asked sadly. "Forgive me, I didn't mean it... It's a wrong question... We aren't getting much done today, are we?" I decided to change the subject.

"Yes, you are right," she replied and, picking up another glass of liquid air, poured it onto the table.

It happened so quickly, I didn't get my hand off the table. Some liquid air spilled on my fingers and hissed as it evaporated. I felt the burn.

"God! What have I done?!" the girl exclaimed. "I am so sorry."

She rushed to the first aid wall case, pulled out ointment, cotton, and bandages.

Her face was filled with such sincere dismay, and she took such great care of me, I was more than rewarded for the earlier disappointment.

The door to Nora's father's office opened, and he looked in.

"Well, Nora, is it ready?" Engelbrecht asked.

"We didn't finish," Nora replied. "Mr. Klimenko injured his hand."

"Nothing serious I hope?" the scientist asked.

"It's nothing," I replied quickly.

"Be careful," he said instructively. "I'm waiting!" The door closed.

My hand was safely bandaged, and we settled at the table. Nora sighed.

"I decided not to work anymore," she said, "but my father is waiting. He needs this."

"Does your father know about everything having to do with Mr. Bailey?" I asked.

"I'd like to know that myself. I want to talk to my father and ask him about it. When we prepared for this ill-fated expedition, father told me we were going to explore the Great Northern Passage. We landed not far from the Yana delta. We were told the pilots who traveled with us on the icebreaker discovered the rest of our route to the east was blocked by ice. We had to spend the winter. Everything was unloaded from the ship. There was a lot of stuff, much more than we would have needed for just one winter. I saw piles of large boxes. But I don't know what was in them. We settled down for the winter. Some of the crew remained on the ship, including two professors – one radio engineer, and an astronomer."

"Why did you need an astronomer for the polar expedition?"

"I don't know. These two professors had some kind of a falling out with Mr. Bailey during the trip. They kept to themselves and sometimes talked to each other quietly. One morning, when I stepped out of my tent to help out with unloading, I saw the ship was gone. I was told it's been carried off into the ocean in the middle of the night, with those professors still on it. The astronomer's body was found later – it was brought to the shore by the sea. The radio engineer must have perished with the ship. I was very surprised. There was no storm that night. I asked Mr. Bailey about it, but he laughed – he could laugh about it! – And told me I must have slept very soundly and missed the storm. 'But the sea is completely calm,' I said, pointing at the ocean. 'There are no big waves this time of year,' Mr. Bailey replied. 'The ice floes reduce the swell. There was a great gust of wind. It broke the ship's anchor chain and carried it off into the ocean.'."

Eleonora paused, recording something in a notebook and watching a beaker on a scale. Then she spoke up again, "Something else strange – we unloaded from the ship two airplanes with large payload. We didn't need them for the winter. As I discovered later, they were used to transport everything inland. The airplane took everything – box by box. Father explained to me Mr. Bailey had a change in plans. With the ship gone, he decided to conduct geological research on the continent. Transportation continued despite winter weather. Some of the cargo was sent off on vehicles equipped with skis. All this work took several months and cost several lives. We replaced the lost sailors with Yakuts who sometimes wandered into our camp by accident. All in all, it was a very deserted spot, and we worked without interruptions – far from prying eyes. Finally, father and I flew to the new site. It was a completely deserted mountain country. Drilling machines were digging through the cold soil like moles. I know little about machines, but I was struck by their power. You should have seen them in action – these amazing machines! From time to time new machines and materials were delivered by airplane. Apparently, Mr. Bailey had a way to communicate with the outside world. The underground settlement was constructed with miraculous speed.

"None of it suggested geological research. But Mr. Bailey told me he found uranium ore and was planning to mine for radium. Besides, he decided to extract nitrogen from air and set up liquid air manufacturing. After all, I wasn't really interested in Mr. Bailey's work. I started helping my father in his scientific work fairly early and traveled with him a great deal. I wasn't afraid of all the moving around. But I'd never lived in this kind of wilderness. My father had great offers from respectable companies. I asked him what made him accept Mr. Bailey's offer. Father told me Mr. Bailey offered him a hundred thousand pounds for one year of work. An entire fortune! 'I want to provide for your future,' father said. A year passed, by father continued working for Mr. Bailey. At one point, I asked father whether it was time for us to go home. He was taken aback a little and replied he was very busy (at the time, he was experimenting with converting oxygen into hydrogen by using electricity) and didn't want to interrupt his work. 'The laboratories are wonderful here, and it's so quiet — you won't find that anywhere in the world. It's great to work here,' he justified his decision. I was a little disappointed. Then father said, if I wanted, I could leave and stay with an aunt. My mother died when I was little. I didn't want to leave my father and stayed in the underground city."

"What made your father stay after all? The pay?"

"I don't want you to think my father is greedy," Nora replied hurriedly. "No one declines a large sum, if offered. But he wouldn't have stayed just for the money."

"Then why was he taken aback when you asked him when you would leave?"

"I don't know. Maybe because he held science above my interests. At least, that's what I thought at the time. But now, after what I heard from you, it occurs to me my father didn't stay with Mr. Bailey... entirely of his own free will. Or... But I don't want to think about it... I must find out for certain. I'll talk to my father."

"What if you find out Mr. Bailey is keeping your father prisoner?"

Nora's face turned stern and determined.

"Then — Then I'll fight. and you'll help me!" I held out my good hand to her, and Nora shook it.

"Nora, how is your work?" we heard Engelbrecht's voice again.

"Ready in five minutes," she said, returning to the test tubes.

"You know what?" I said, when the door to the study closed. "Stop breaking glasses and spilling liquid air. It's childish. We'll work as we have before. We mustn't cause the slightest suspicion."

Nora nodded silently and became absorbed in work.

That night, I was alone in my room. Nikola was gone. Apparently, Bailey decided to separate us. It was a great blow to me. I have grown used and even attached to the Yakut. Besides, I needed him to help me with my plans. Sooner or later, the struggle between Bailey and me was bound to come out into the open. I didn't give up the idea of escape for a moment, or the idea of at least warning our government about the danger.

Nikola returned three days later. He was as cheerful as ever and childishly carefree. His severe surroundings made him tougher, and he became used to life's troubles.

"Nikola!" I greeted him happily.

"Hello, comrade!" he replied. He sat down on the floor with his legs crossed and started humming, "Nikola was on

83

water and bread, not too bad. Nikola had little to eat, but some time to sing and sit."

"Nikola, you know how to rhyme!" I was surprised.

"I don't know," he replied. "My kids go to school, they know lots of songs. I heard."

"How is Ivan?"

"Ivan's alive. He was with me. He is off to work."

Bailey must have decided my "accomplices" didn't require severe punishment. Or rather, he kept them as additional workforce.

"We're in trouble, Nikola," I said. "Would you try and run away with me again?"

"Wind in the way. Not bad. If you run, I'll run."

XII.   A NEW ACQUAINTANCE

Bailey must have assumed the lesson he taught me and the sight of his terrible "pantheon" completely knocked the idea of escape out of my head and made me accept my position. In any case, I was given greater freedom after our excursion. I was given access to the areas of the settlement, from which I had been barred in the past. I still could not get into the engine room or the arsenal where the large weapons were stored. However, I made a new useful acquaintance with the local radio operator.

It was an elderly Scot who spoke decent German. At one time he worked in Germany, at a radio equipment factory. Contrary to the stereotypical notion about the English, Luke was very talkative, which was helpful. He also turned out to be an avid chess player, and since I was an advanced player, he made it his life's goal to beat me, even though he was a much weaker player himself.

Chess brought us together. In the evenings, when Luke's shift was over, he invariably came to me with his cast iron chess set in the shape of figurines of English king and queen, knights that looked like Don Quixote, and pawns resembling medieval soldiers.

Luke soon became absorbed in the game, and when he moved his pawns, he thumped them so hard against the board, as if real soldiers marched across a bridge. He said, "Infantry, ahead! Like this? Here we go!" I pretended to ponder his move and asked him a few questions, systematically whittling out of him whatever I wanted to know. I found out Luke was an old bachelor with no family or friend; he didn't feel like going home and stayed with Bailey of his own free will, attracted by good salary and unlimited access to gin, of which Luke was very fond.

"Home is where gin is," Luke said. "But I drink intelligently. I am always clean as a whistle at work."

I took this new information into account, and always had a bottle of gin I received from an obliging bar keeper waiting when Luke came to visit. Out of business considerations, Bailey believed it necessary to satisfy the wishes of all his willing and unwilling workers as much as possible, to alleviate their longing for freedom and keep from causing unrest.

To reach my goal, I even decided to sacrifice my reputation as an advanced chess player. From time to time, I lost the last round to Luke. When gin and joy of victory loosened his tongue, I proceeded with important questions.

I admit it wasn't entirely honest with respect to Luke. But was Bailey treating me honestly? I decided all methods were acceptable In my struggle with him. It was military reconnaissance within the limits of my conditions and circumstance. My goals were more important than the ethics of a casual acquaintance.

"What news on the radio today, Luke?" I asked with a yawn.

Luke told me the news. That was how I discovered my friend, young scientist, Shiryaev, was appointed to lead the expedition in my place. Despite the beginning of winter, the expedition had set out. However, the storms and high winds forced them to return to Verkhoyansk. After the group's report about the weather, an order was received to postpone the expedition until spring and, in the meantime, conduct meteorological observations of the area.

This news made me both glad and sad. Shiryaev was more cautious than me – he did not wish to risk the lives of his companions and his own, and thus, avoided the fate Bailey prophesized for him. I was happy for my friend. But this also meant I would not get any help from the outside until spring. *Just as well*, I reasoned with myself. *Bailey will kill anyone who carelessly approaches his underground domain.* Fighting him required the strength of the entire state.

But in order for them to succeed, I had to warn the government to treat the task with utmost seriousness. Perhaps, I could spend the winter to somehow establish connection with the outside world.

I decided to be patient while continuing my "spying".

Luke and I became closer. Once, at the moment of frankness, he told me a little about the *Arctic*. Luke was one of the few who knew its secret, even though Bailey didn't tell Luke everything about his plans. According to Luke, the *Arctic* had been sent loose in the ocean in the northern direction, its engines running full speed, to stage a collision. Bailey had no intention to move further east. He simply wanted to "pick up a few useful minerals in your country without getting into any nonsense with the government."

"Oh, he's very clever, Mr. Bailey is!" Luke said almost admiringly. "Businessman! What did you expect? You have treasures lying about and wasted, and he turned it into money. Mr. Bailey did a good job tricking you!" Luke laughed. "The engineer fired up the engine, the helmsman fixed the wheel and off it went! When the *Arctic* started moving, everyone jumped off into a motor boat, and the ship kept going. Neat, eh?"

"Was there anyone left on the ship?" I asked Luke.

"No one," he replied.

I was afraid of making him suspicious and did not ask him about the fate of two vanished professors. After some hesitation, I asked a cautious question, "Did everything go well, with no accidents or casualties?"

"A few people died when moving from the shore to here, and we lost a couple of scientists. They say, those two went hunting and didn't come back."

"Did you look for them?"

"I think so. No one had time. Everyone was swamped. Winter was coming."

Either Luke didn't tell me everything, or he didn't know more himself. In any case, I could not count on him for help. He clearly did not feel too friendly toward my government. He was a typical mediocre servant. His ideals were limited to getting paid well, drinking gin, and setting aside money to return home and buy a little house, where he could live without having to work much.

One time I told him I was very interested in radio but, unfortunately, had no opportunities to become acquainted with this remarkable invention.

"It's very simple," Luke replied. "Come join me at the radio station during the night shift, and I'll show you."

I took advantage of this invitation and became a frequent visitor.

I was incredibly moved when, after many months, I heard the familiar voice of a radio announcer, "We bring you the latest news..."

"And now, comrades, the winter forecast from our meteorologists. We have some good news for our winter vacationers – they won't have to freeze. Scientists promise a very warm winter this year, more so than last year."

Of course! I thought. Mr. Bailey's fans create a kind of aerial Gulfstream. Warm air currents are moving north from the equator and raising the temperature.

"South of Africa, however, as well as South America and Australia are seeing significant drops in temperature," the announcer continued.

The breath of the South Pole! I replied to the announcer in my mind. If only I could call out to him from here, across thousands of kilometers and tell him there was no reason to be happy about the warm winter, since it signaled a tremendous catastrophe threatening all of humanity!

"And now let's have some music. Our orchestra will now perform *Minuet* by Boccherini."

The sounds of a light, elegant minuet filled the room. But the music only made me feel worse. Life went on out there. People worked, enjoyed their entertainments, and lived as usual, not knowing of the danger hanging over their heads.

I took off the headphones. Luke was absorbed in receiving a transmission, converting dashes and dots of the Morse code into letters. He quickly recorded a telegram. Every morning, these telegrams were turned in to Mr. Bailey.

He finally looked up from his work, although he kept his headphones on, and asked, "Anything interesting?"

"Yes. But I used to receive these channels on my radio at home. I'd like to know, how to transmit as well as receive. Do you have a transmitter?"

Perhaps, I was too suspicious and cautious, but I thought I saw a hint of alarm in Luke's face.

"Do you wish to send a message to your friends and family?" he asked with a smile. "Yes, we have a transmitting station, but we don't use it. We don't want to reveal our location."

I believed him then. But soon I discovered he didn't tell me the truth. Once, I came to the radio station later than usual and found him transmitting.

"Did you decide to reveal your location?" I said with a naïve smile. "Did I catch you red-handed?"

Like frowned but then forced a laugh.

"Are you spying on me?" he said jokingly, but his joke made my heart ache.

"How silly!" I replied. "Whatever for?" I pretended to be offended and said, "I can leave if I'm in your way."

"Stay," Luke replied. "I didn't lie to you – our big transmitter remains silent. But this... This isn't intended for any station in the world, except one. This station uses short waves well below the range used by most stations. This way, the transmission can be kept secret. I am talking about business operations!" he explained. "Listen, Mr. Klimenko, I told you as much as I did because you are my friend. But you mustn't tell anyone you saw me transmitting. And don't come here at this time. It's a professional secret."

I reassured Luke and returned to my room. This latest discovery convinced me Bailey had allies in the outside world. This made him even more dangerous. Luke was apparently losing his trust in me. Had he not been afraid to lose a chess partner, he probably would have barred me from the radio station altogether. I had to be doubly cautious.

XIII.   CALM BEFORE THE STORM

"At the lab, we breathe very clean, oxygen-saturated air. And yet, I'm missing something," Nora admitted. "Some sort of 'air vitamins' I suppose. Perhaps, we lack the smells or earth, pine trees, the sight of the sky, even if it's this gloomy northern sky. I truly enjoy the fresh air only when I'm up here."

We were standing on a balcony around a small ledge in a gap in the outside of the crater.

There were several such balconies on the outward slope of the mountain. They were connected to the top three levels through a series of sloping tunnels. Each tunnel had an elevator. The balconies could be used for observation and guarding. But the hurricane-strength wind, sucking anyone who came close into the crater made guarding completely unnecessary. The privileged dwellers of the upper levels used the balconies to breathe "real" air and look at the sky.

With Bailey's gracious permission, Nora picked out one balcony to have at her sole disposal. She kept the key to the entrance to the tunnel leading to the balcony. Bailey himself had the second key. This door was not far from her room, and Nora could get up to the balcony at any time. She spent a lot of time there and loved to "talk to the stars". It was a very secluded spot because the rock outcroppings obscured the balcony from the other balconies, and no one could see what took place there.

The ledge dropped off steeply. Mountains around us were covered in snow. Stars sparkled in the dark sky. There was no wind.

"Air vitamins... I like how you said that," I replied. "I can no longer smell the earth, everything is covered in snow. But I can smell the pine. And something else, like smoke from somewhere far away."

"Smoke means dwellings, people..."

"Who very much enjoy the 'air vitamins'. And Mr. Bailey wants to deprive them of all this!"

"Look!"

I turned to the north. A pale column of light rose from the horizon – higher and higher, all the way to the zenith. The pillar turned from milky to pale-blue and then light-green. The top of the pillar turned pink, and, suddenly, broad bands stretched away from it like branches from a tree. A sheet of light shimmering with incredible delicate, translucent hues across the full spectrum rose from the horizon. The polar night was enchanting. A silent symphony of color played out before us across the sky. The colors flowed like sounds from an orchestra, sometimes flaring up in a powerful chord, and sometimes pausing tremulously in a pianissimo of barely visible hues.

"The world is so beautiful!" Nora said with some sadness in her voice.

I took her hand in a fur glove. Nora seemed not to notice it and continued to stand motionless, gazing at the panorama of mountain ranges and valleys before us. The white snow reflected heavenly lights and constantly changed colors, turning blue and pink. It was the kind of beauty that captivated one for life. Solitude... Emptiness... The chorus of beautiful, but mute lights... It was as if we were transported into some completely different, fantastic world. And there, beyond the mountains, in the south-east and south-west roiled the human anthill.

"Ms. Engelbrecht, have you talked to you father?" I broke the silence.

Nora seemed to return to Earth from the interstellar expanses.

"I have," she replied, lowering her head.

"How did your conversation go?" Nora looked up tiredly.

"How did it go?" she repeated, as if she didn't hear me clearly. "My father kissed my forehead the way he used to do when he put me to bed as a little girl and said, 'Sleep well, little one.' And I went to my room. Father! My dear father, from whom I'd never been away even for a single day, seemed to leave me. He became distant, incomprehensible, and even... scary... I can no longer treat him with the same trust."

We were silent once again. The heavenly hymn of Northern lights grew and broadened, like a powerful pipe organ made of light, cold, soundless, beautiful, and alien to everything that moved us.

***

The days that followed were boring and monotonous. Nora and I continued to work at the lab, but the girl had lost her old enthusiasm. In the past, Nora took great joy in earning her father's approval. Now he did everything mechanically, like an unwilling servant merely earning her daily bread. She suffered deeply. Her beautiful complexion turned pale, her eyes sunk in, she became noticeably thinner and more absentminded. She dropped beakers frequently and often made mistake. I saw Professor Engelbrecht only rarely, but I noticed a change in him too. His face looked more haggard, older, and darker.

In the evenings after work, Nora and I sometimes came out to our balcony to admire Northern lights, to breathe the "air vitamins", and, most importantly, to talk. Nora felt lonely in her grief, and I was the only person, in whose company she found moral support.

The wind over the crater has been quiet for several days. It was uncommonly still.

"Mr. Bailey must have decided to give the air a break," I joke.

"Yes, but that's nothing to joke about," Nora replied. "We are moving to a new method for concentrating the air. In the winter, entire clouds of snow dust got blown in, which made our work more complicated. The snow removed from the fan took up too much space and demanded too much work to clean. See that mountain? It's artificial. It doesn't melt even in the summer. A year from now it can be as tall as Montblanc. Father combined all the powers of chemistry and electricity and found new ways to absorb the air and split it into its components. Alas, the process is bound to move even faster now. Soon, Earth will begin to suffocate, like in a giant asthma attack."

"Nora, let's get out of here!" I suddenly said. The girl looked at me.

"Hold hands and jump off this balcony?" she asked jokingly. It was almost coquettish. Before I could answer, Nora continued in the same tone, "We probably wouldn't crash. We would roll down and fall into the soft snow. And then go that way..."

I took a careful look at where Nora was pointing. Indeed, it was a viable escape route! There was no tube here.

The winding canyon would protect us from the wind, even if it were raised by the new "wind god" Bailey.

"Don't joke like that. Nora, this is a great way to get out," I expressed my idea out loud. "It's a little high. If you are reluctant, I'll go by myself."

Something like fear flickered across Nora's eyes.

"You would leave me alone? I won't let you."

"Are you following Mr. Bailey's orders?"

"I won't let you go," Nora continued, "because you might be caught like the first time, and my intercession won't help you. Besides, you are not equipped for that kind of journey. Your sacrifice will be in vain. Only a man born in this frozen desert can set out on such a trip – a Yakut, like your Nikola. Why don't you send him? He fits the task to perfection. And soon, we'll be showered with missiles. And we'll 'die like heroes'," she said with bitter irony.

"Our troops will be warned, and, perhaps, we'll manage to avoid this honorable death. Maybe, once under siege, Mr. Bailey realizes it's useless to struggle and surrender," I tried to soften the gloomy prediction. "That's not a bad suggestion. I'm prepared to take a risk, but you are right – Nikola will do it better."

"Will Nikola agree?"

"Nikola! You don't know him. He has a heart of gold. He looked death in the eye so many times, our project is unlikely to frighten or surprise him."

I felt a little better. Nora too cheered up a bit. The circle of hopelessness seemed to break. We had a specific plan. We discussed it in detail, which distracted Nora from dark thoughts.

Nikola and I met in my room, and I whispered, "Nikola, I found a good place to escape. Can you make your way to

Verkhoyansk? I'll give you warm clothes, a revolver, and a sack of crackers and smoked meat."

"And you?" Nikola asked quietly.

"We can't go together. We are more likely to get caught. If you don't make it, I'll try for it. Although, if you don't want to go alone…"

"Why not one? I'm bored. Why Verkhoyansk?"

"You'll take a letter. Will you go?"

"Yes," Nikola replied.

"I want you to think carefully, Nikola, I am not forcing you. If you get caught, you won't get away with it so easily. You might get killed."

"Bear might kill, people might kill," Nikola formulated fatalistically. "When go? Now?"

"No, we'll wait a little. We must think about it carefully and prepare everything. We'll have sunlight soon, winter is almost over."

"No need for sun. I can see. Want to go now."

I had a tough time talking Nikola out of an immediate trip. We started getting ready. I gave him my own fur jacket and boots. I could say Nikola "stole" them from me. Nora helped me get a revolver. All that was left was to gather the food. That was the hardest part. At dinner, we had to surreptitiously sneak away bits of bread and crackers. Nikola also stored away food, but I didn't let him cut his portions – he was going to need his strength.

Nora's way to get more food was to suddenly develop a huge appetite. Soon, the bag I kept under my pillow filled up. Nikola could set out in a few days.

However, we had to make sure I remained beyond suspicion. If Nikola didn't make it to Verkhoyansk and died, I would have to go – I had to be careful until then.

XIV.   MR. KLIMENKO'S "TRICKS"

Following my advice, a few days before the planned escape, Nikola started telling his work mates he was bored with the underground settlement and decided to get out.

"Comrade Klimenko doesn't know. If he knew, I'd be in trouble," Nikola said.

Everyone tried talking Nikola out of it and scared him with terrible punishments, but Nikola insisted: beast kills, man kills – doesn't matter. He couldn't stand it anymore.

There was the risk one of the people who knew about Nikola's secret would tell Bailey about the impending escape. But we had to take that risk. He said he wanted to repeat his first attempt and try escaping through the outlet tube. Had anyone told Bailey about Nikola's plans, Bailey would pay no attention, knowing for certain such an attempt was doomed to fail. That way, we were prepared.

Finally came the day, or rather, the night of escape. Nikola and I agreed he would come to the balcony, fully dressed and ready to go after everyone fell asleep.

Nora and I waited at the appointed hour. It was a fairly dark night. Only a few pale streaks ran across the sky – probably the distant, faint beams of a floodlight.

Time passed, and Nikola wasn't there. I started worrying, when the door to the balcony opened, and Nikola came out.

"Why are you so late?" I asked. Nikola smiled broadly.

"I'm clever," he replied. "I stayed at work in the tube and waited for everyone to go. Then I walked back-to-front to leave tracks."

Nikola was an avid tracker. He knew how animals confused hunters by mixing their tracks and decided to use the animal wisdom, adding some of his human smarts to it. By walking backwards, he left fresh tracks in the remains of snow and trash in the pipe, so, should there be an investigation, it would look, as if he followed the tube to the outlet.

"Well, good luck!" I said anxiously, giving him the letter.

"All right," he replied. He then looked down and said, "A bit high, though. All right. Soft down there. Farewell, comrade!" He shook my hand and nodded to Nora, "Farewell, lady."

He then boldly stepped over the balcony's iron railing over the abyss, lowered himself, hung on the edge for a second, and let go.

I leaned over, peering into the gloom. Nikola's body was receding rapidly as it fell. He would fall at least forty meters before reaching the snow-covered slope.

Finally, his feet touched the snow, and his entire body fell into the snow drift, as if he jumped into water. I strained my eyes, but saw nothing. Nikola vanished in the snow mass. Did he crash? Did he faint? Rippling green-pink sheets of northern lights moved across the sky, shedding uncertain, tremulous light on the snow. I saw the hole Nikola's body made in the snow, but still didn't see him.

"Look, look, something's moving down there..." Nora said anxiously.

"Where? I can't see anything. You are imagining it."

The flaring lights made the shadows move, turning them thicker here and paler there.

"Not there! Further below! Much further!"

I looked below the spot where he fell and saw something small moving in the snow two dozen paces away.

"It's an arm!" Nora said, since her eyesight was better than mine.

I strained my eyes and finally saw she was right, and the thing showing from under the snow was indeed Nikola's arm. His body pierced the fluffy layer of fresh snow on top, slid a few dozen meters down, and he was now digging a hole to get out. We saw his other arm and his fur hat. He climbed halfway out. Then he leaned and finally pushed himself out all the way, and turned to face us, waving both arms and fur mittens.

I barely held back a triumphant shout.

Nikola waved to us one more time, stretched out on one side, and rolled down the slope until he reached the bottom of the chasm, turning into a barely discernible dot. Then, flopping and getting stuck in the snow, he crawled to the outlet from the gap. He had no skis – we couldn't get any – but that didn't hold him back. "I'll make some," he told me.

Nikola was going to be all right! He was used to the harsh life in the "cursed country", just like the animals he hunted. As long as he didn't end up in Bailey's clutches, he could manage the nature and four-legged foes.

The lights faded. We lost sight of Nikola, but kept looking out into the dark abyss for a long time.

"It's time to go. We can't stay here long," Nora said.

"Yes, let's go," I replied, finally looking away. "Tomorrow is retribution day. Mr. Bailey will probably bring me in for an interrogation. Nora, I'd like to ask you. Do you have a second revolver?"

"What for?"

"If Bailey decides I am guilty of Nikola's escape, I'll put a bullet into Bailey."

Nora thought about it.

"I don't know... I don't have another revolver. My father might. If I manage to get it, I'll bring it to you tomorrow. Come to the lab earlier."

I shook her hand thankfully. Yes, Nora was a woman of character. She wasn't afraid to become an accomplice in the escape or help in the possible assassination I was planning.

I slept badly. I just dosed off around two in the morning, there was a loud knock on the door. I dressed quickly and asked who it was.

I heard William's voice. *Right! Bailey already knows, and he wants to question me,* I decided and opened the door. William came in, accompanied by two armed men. Despite myself, I studied their faces – handsome and energetic. Two gentlemen walked up to me and searched me. At that moment, I was very glad I didn't have time to get another revolver from Nora. Then William and his helpers searched my room thoroughly and expertly. Fortunately, I had nothing compromising in there. Having finished with the search, the men took me to Bailey's study.

He greeted me with a storm of indignation.

"More of your tricks!" he shouted, shaking his fists at me. "You can't live with my trading with Mars and violating your trade regulations? Oh yes, Mr. Bailey is a criminal! He should go before the Supreme Court! Tell me, please! Mr. Bailey will take the air away from the Russian workers, and the air will be dispensed in rations through cooperatives and unions! Ha-ha-ha! Isn't that so? The intrigues of English imperialists? Oh, I know what you think. And I think you'll have to take your place in the pantheon. The pedestal has been waiting for you a long time."

I was prepared for this attack and played my role well. I waited for Bailey to finish and said calmly and with sincere surprise, "What's the matter, Mr. Bailey? I don't understand. I don't think I'd earned your reproach. I'd been working hard at the lab and haven't done anything wrong."

"Lies! You know exactly what I'm talking about. Where's Nikola?"

"I don't know. He didn't come back tonight. I thought he was at work or maybe he was being punished for something and sent into solitary confinement."

"Lies! Lies!" Bailey shouted. "It's your tricks! Get me the workers who were with Nikola!"

The workers came. The Yakuts confirmed Nikola mentioned escaping a few days earlier and talked about missing his freedom. Nikola said he was afraid to tell Klimenko about it, because Klimenko would get angry. But they didn't believe he seriously intended to run, so they didn't report him.

This testimony cooled Bailey's anger somewhat. My lack of connection with the escape was supported by an entire group of witnesses.

"I don't believe you, and I don't believe them," Bailey said. "You're in cahoots with each other! You are covering for each other."

Suddenly turning into an objective judge he concluded, I cannot judge you without evidence. The investigation will continue. Meanwhile, you are all under suspicion. Go."

I returned to my room, happy everything had worked out so well. I hoped they wouldn't think of examining the valley. But Nikola's trick with reverse tracks was bound to point the search in the wrong direction.

In the morning, when I came to the lab, Nora whispered to me, "I couldn't find the revolver."

"Just as well," I replied. "Mr. Bailey is not that easy to kill. I have already been questioned."

I told Nora bout the events of the night before. She listened to me very carefully.

"I hope they don't find any tracks in the valley," I concluded.

"Don't worry," she replied. "I went to the balcony early in the morning. There's been a snowstorm and it hid the tracks. I'm afraid the same storm may have trapped Nikola himself..."

"Nikola will be all right," I reassured her. "He'll lie in wait somewhere and sleep in the snow just as well as in bed."

Luke came to see me the same evening with a bundle under his arm.

"What's that? New chess?" I asked.

"Chess and something else," he replied, unwrapping it. "It's a radio. I made it for you. Mr. Bailey ordered to keep you out of the radio station. I know you are very fond of listening to your state radio. So, I decided to make you a little present. You won't be quite so bored."

I was ready to kiss Luke for his "little present". Luke had no idea what a huge favor he was doing me. To reward Luke, I let him checkmate me twice that evening.

He then personally set up the radio, tested it and said, "Listen to your Moscow."

Having wished me good night, he left, and I started listening.

XV.   THE WORLD SUFFOCATES...

Weeks followed weeks. I continued to remain under Mr. Bailey's suspicion, but he didn't bother me. Apparently, he was becoming convinced of my innocence. Gradually, I stopped worrying about my safety. However, the news I received from the radio was very worrisome. The lack of air was becoming more perceptible. Not just scientists but even ordinary people were noticing the reduction in the atmospheric pressure.

Those living in the mountainous areas were the first to feel the thinning air, and many of them were forced to come down into the valleys. In the valleys, the lack of air was impacting the chronically ill. Asthma patients started dying during their attacks; tuberculosis patients suffocated, tried breathing harder, thus accelerating the process and causing internal bleeding.

Machines designed to operate under ordinary atmospheric pressure refused to work. Airplane engines skipped even at low altitudes. Pistons and pumps went out of whack. All of this together upset manufacturing and transportation.

To make things worse, cold weather swept in, accompanied by storms of very odd nature. Tornadoes rushed about like messengers of death. It was as if someone's evil hand rushed to strip Earth of its atmosphere by twisting air streams into coils and tossing them beyond the clouds. Icy streams of cold descended on Earth from the interstellar space. Earth was cooling. Devoid of a significant part of its thick atmospheric coat, Earth started surrendering its inner warmth to space.

Judging by greater-than-expected stores of air, the catastrophe was approaching faster than one might expect.

I asked Nora how her father explained all these ominous events. Nora replied that, apparently, her father and Mr. Bailey were somewhat surprised by all this.

"Father even wanted to ask your advice," Nora said. "This has more to do with your specialty."

I had the honor of being invited to Engelbrecht's office. Bailey was there as well. He wasn't at all upset by what was going on in the world, on the contrary – the air merchant was pleasantly excited, like a gambler certain of his hand.

Our meeting lasted for quite some time. We made a series of calculations and concluded the air stored in the underground city comprised a too-small part of the atmosphere, and its withdrawal from the total amount of air surrounding Earth could not have caused such catastrophic events.

"What is the matter then?" Bailey asked, looking at Engelbrecht and me.

I finally felt like an equal! Mr. Bailey needed my opinion! I assumed an intellectual air and expressed my opinion, "Mr. Bailey's fans changed the wind directions around the globe, thus altering the 'tautness' of the atmosphere: the air is denser where the usual air currents overlapped with the artificial one and thinner where the air currents oppose each other. Thus, the difference in maximum and minimum atmospheric pressure increased and with it – the cyclone activity. Colliding cyclones are drawing the air upwards, above their normal area of influence. Thus, the normal air circulation is violated not only longitudinally but also lattitudinally."

I noticed Bailey and Engelbrecht listened to my explanation with great attention.

"Perhaps, this doesn't entirely correspond to the reality," I concluded, "but, in general, I think my assumption is correct. My main idea is, by upsetting the normal air circulation, Mr. Bailey's fans drew forces of nature into the game. You, Mr. Bailey, are much like Doctor Faust, who had summoned the 'spirit of Earth' but couldn't handle it."

Bailey treated the comparison with Faust favorably. He chuckled and said, "Faust was a very impractical man. Let the 'spirits of Air' play and be free. It's all about using this in the most advantageous way."

Our meeting ended.

The radio brought more news. Faced with the terrible catastrophe, the struggle for survival became more brutal. The strong were not going to survive but were bound to outlive the weak. Of course, the strongest in the capitalist world were the wealthiest.

Was it Bailey who supplied them with canned air, or did the wealthiest of the world start producing liquid air for themselves to keep from dying of air starvation? In any case, they now held this new, most valuable commodity in their hands. Liquid air made a triumphant entry on the market, bringing down all other valuables. Liquid air was sold in special packages protected from explosions and evaporation.

With this new currency, the wealthy started buying food and all manner of canned goods. Apparently, the cooling Earth could no longer bear fruit and grain. Agriculture was doomed. Only those who collected the greatest stores of food, water, air, and warmth would survive the longest. Above-ground construction ground to a halt. In some areas people were already moving underground like moles. It was warmer, and breathing in the hermetically sealed apartments was easier, by gradually using the liquid air stores.

It was amazing how quickly events unfolded out there, far away from our settlement!

This feverishly selfish self-preservation unfolded before the eyes of ordinary workers, who were becoming anxious in many areas. Citing the wind direction, traveling from all corners of the world toward the icy wastes of Siberia, all of the media sources became convinced the terrible catastrophe descending upon the world had been caused by Moscow communists who decided to bring the world to its knees.

The world was overcome by madness. Europe and America frantically armed themselves for the war with the "tormentors of humankind".

The wealthy continued with their politics. The workers refused to accept monetary payments and demanded their wages in liquid air instead. Business owners were forced to yield, but they set very low rations – liquid air was handed out in special "thermal" canisters in a way the workers couldn't make any stores. Since the air was already growing sparse in some areas (particularly in Western Europe, Africa, and America), the workers had no choice but to work for the right to breathe. Masks similar to gas masks became available for sale, and more people appeared in them in public. Since the masks weren't equipped with radios like our suits, people could only communicate with gestures.

Members of the Fascist movement openly said it was for the better since people would have fewer chances to conspire. Upper classes eventually purchased portable radios as did the police.

Nevertheless, dissidents managed to get their message across using leaflets. Struggle between classes intensified and came into stark contrast. The strain reached extreme levels. "Air rebellions" flared up in various places. Crowds stormed stores of liquid air and destroyed them. There was bloodshed.

I stayed up overnight listening to the radio. There was plenty to drive me to desperation. Even Luke had lost his usual carefree air. He still stopped by to see me after his shifts, but without chess.

"Bad business," he grumbled. "What's the point of the money I had set aside while working for Mr. Bailey? Money is worthless. Suppose I can buy a really nice little house for a canister or even a bottle of liquid air. But why do I want it? Earth is suffocating."

"Whose fault is it?" I ask irritably.

"Alarmists and black market merchants," he replied.

"And what brought on the alarm?"

"Nonsense. There's plenty of air for us. Mr. Bailey can't take away all of it."

No, I couldn't bring Luke to my side. Even faced with a world-wide tragedy, he refused to change – his house and his own welfare were still his highest priorities. Luke was starting to bug me. I pretended to have a headache or too much work and tried to send him off quickly, so I could return to my radio.

My nerves became completely unhinged. I kept dropping things at work. Nora was also feeling poorly. Her beautiful complexion was gone. Pale and thin, she often sat still staring at the same spot.

"Everything's dying," she whispered quietly. "Here we are breathing pure, oxygen-saturated air, and out there, people are dying, children are suffocating… And none of them knows why…"

The day came, when I decided to reply to her as I probably should have a long time ago.

"They will know," I said. "Nikola obviously didn't make it. I leave tonight. Mr. Bailey is too busy with his American 'competition' and new construction. The surveillance is lax, and I think I can make it."

Nora turned toward me like a sleepwalker and said almost without a sound, "You'll die as Nikola did." Her face was hopeless, almost indifferent.

"So what? Death is better than this terrible inaction while thousands of people die."

"Yes, death is better than this…" Nora said just as quietly.

That day she said good bye to me without her usual smile. Every day her smile paled, turning sadder until it finally faded away like her rosy coloring.

"Farewell," I said holding out my hand.

"Farewell," she replied.

"Will you… come to see me off? To the balcony?"

"I will," she replied. "Where? To the balcony? Ah, yes, yes…" And she walked off with her head bowed.

XVI.   THE GAME BEGINS

I left the girl to her thoughts and quietly walked out of the lab. Having returned to my room, I tiredly dropped onto a chair. I felt exhausted. Snippets of thoughts rushed through my mind. Nikola was dead. The world was dying. Nora was dying... or was likely to soon go mad.

Habitually, automatically, I put on the radio headphones.

I listened to the national news. There was no music, no singing – only the endless stream of information about the suffocating Earth. It wasn't quite as bad as abroad. There was no animal-like struggle for the last breath of air. The government did all it could to reduce panic and save the people. But what was there to do? Peasants scattered through distant villages were in the worst position. Was death the only option?

I was about to take off the headphones when I heard the news, which made me hold my breath.

"Courage, comrades! Today, the government received extremely important information, which can radically change the situation..."

Raising his voice, the announcer said clearly, "Hello! Hello! Ay-Toyon's Nostril exists!" Then he added in his ordinary voice, "You might not understand this address, comrades, but soon you will all know about Ay-Toyon's Nostril and literally breathe a sigh of relief."

I was the first one to breathe the sigh of relief.

"Ay-Toyon's Nostril exists!" These were the code words I asked to speak on the radio in case Nikola managed to get my letter to Shiryaev, my replacement. Shiryaev, in turn, was supposed to send my report to Moscow. Nikola was alive, and the government knew all about Mr. Bailey's underground city!

I quickly got dressed and ran to the balcony. Nora wasn't there yet. The sky was singing with lights. But this song no longer felt as cold and alien to me. I too wanted to sing and scream. I started singing for the first time after my capture, "Sadness follows every joy, but joy comes following the sadness..."

"You are mad!" I heard Nora's voice behind me. "Someone might hear you. Singing in this cold?! You'll ruin your throat."

"Yes, I am mad! Let them hear! So what if I ruin my throat? Nikola is alive! Ay-Toyon's Nostril exists!"

"What's going on, Georgy?" This was the first time Nora called me by my first name.

I grabbed her, picked her up, and twirled her around the balcony.

"You're crazy! Let go of me and tell me what's going on."

"Listen! Everything is great. I received news on the radio. Nikola is alive! He took my letter to the right people. We should expect new developments soon. The stolen air will soon be returned. You and I will probably be blown to smithereens! But that's all right. We'll try to escape at the last moment when we hear the bombers coming. Oh, it will be a great day!"

"Georgy, is that true?" she exclaimed, and her cheeks once again turned pink.

Her joy was as great as mine. However, the girl's glowing face soon darkened. By that time, I could read all the subtleties in its expression. She was thinking about her father.

His behavior remained a dark mystery to her. Then Nora's thoughts turned in a different direction.

"Now you don't have to go on your dangerous journey," she said. "That is good. But, in general, it's too early to celebrate. Mr. Bailey is not that easy to defeat. He'll resist to the last. He is a terrible opponent."

"Nonsense!" I shouted. "One man cannot resist an entire country or the entire world."

"Who knows?" Nora replied. "You can't imagine the terrible weapons of mass destruction Mr. Bailey owns."

"At least there will be a fight instead of a wordless suffocation. Besides, Mr. Bailey has enemies in his own camp. They are few, yes, but they can be more dangerous than enemy armies."

"There are only two of these enemies – you and me," Nora said. "But you are right. We can do a lot. Oh, if only my father!.." She looked down.

Then she straightened out and said firmly, "The time will come when I ask my father directly whether he is my friend or my enemy."

There was a sudden gust of icy wind from below, followed by humming from the crater.

"The fan is back on," Nora said. "Mr. Bailey is in a hurry to process the remaining air. It's cold... Come..."

That night I wished Nora good night, taking with me the memory of her smile, as if I'd seen the sun after a long winter.

I returned to the radio.

The station transmitted the latest government report.

Expedition Chief Shiryaev managed to establish the point of convergence of air currents. The government was

112

preparing a new expedition to establish exact reasons of the unusual air loss at thus and such coordinates.

I smiled at this. I knew Shiryaev was not going anywhere from Verkhoyansk. The honor of discovering the "point of convergence" was given to him following my advice to reduce Mr. Bailey's suspicions in my regard, since he was bound to receive this important information. I could only imagine how mad Mr. Bailey was going to be, when he found out his location was no longer secret. This was bound to look all the more believable since his powerful fans were idle for some time, and expedition members could come near the crater without any risk of being pulled in by the suction.

As usual, the government acted quickly and decisively. Unfortunately, I could tell them nothing about Mr. Bailey's military capability – it was a mystery to me. All I knew was the underground city's population did not exceed five hundred people. Initially, I was surprised by such relatively small number of workers and staff. But Mr. Bailey had automated and streamlined everything to the last detail.

Five hundred people would be but a handful against an entire army! But what weapons were they going to use? All I could do was warn our soldiers in my letter the struggle was bound to be difficult and they must be prepared for the unexpected.

In any case, we didn't have long to wait. The cards have been dealt and the game was on.

***

Mr. Bailey put the settlement on military alert. The garrison prepared for a siege. Watch towers equipped with radars appeared at the edge of the crater. Trap doors opened in its outward slopes revealing embrasures and port holes with thick glass. I had no idea they even existed. Cannons protruded through the embrasures. The giant fans were idle once again, as if inviting the enemy in.

Spring was coming. The weather was quiet and still. After its winter hibernation, the sun started peeking over the horizon, shedding crimson light over the snowy peaks.

The days that followed were filled with strained expectation. The settlement itself didn't show any signs of particular alarm. It appeared as deserted as ever. The labs continued to operate as usual. However, it was clear the labs and workshops were now laboring away for defense purposes. Elevators went up and down all the time, delivering ammo to the hidden weapons. Machines performed the work of entire armies.

Nora and I continued with our duties, turning long columns of Professor Engelbrecht's formulas into new methods for processing our "raw material". We carried out a series of experiments, having no access to the end of synthesis and knowing nothing of their results and purposes. Nora was very worried about this. Perhaps, we were assisting in creating new methods for killing people? Nora's father refused to give any definite answers to her questions.

In the evenings, Nora and I went up to our balcony and watched the empty sky. The aerial messengers were nowhere to be seen (I was certain the new expedition would arrive by air). The main air force contingent was far away from us, and I tried to figure out how quickly they could be moved here. It would be several days at least before airplanes appeared above us, bringing us death, but also salvation to the rest of humankind.

"Look, there are people by the weapons," I told Nora during one of these weary evenings.

I saw shadows moving behind the dark trap doors. Apparently, the radars detected approaching airplanes, and the settlement's defenders were preparing for an aerial attack.

We waited anxiously what would happen next. All was quiet. The sun vanished behind the horizon, and only the waning moon shed dull light on the primitive landscape before us. It was cold, but we didn't want to leave.

At least an hour passed. Suddenly, we were blinded by bright light. A dozen enormous flood lights lit up in a circle along the rim of the crater, lighting the surrounding area for miles. It was as if we were transported from the polar night into a brilliant tropical day at high noon. When our eyes became used to the light, we saw several silver dragonflies in the air. At the same time, we heard the barely perceptible rumbling of the engines.

"They are coming," Nora said anxiously.

"Yes," I replied quietly, watching the small dragonflies turn into swallows, and then into hawks. Closer and closer... One, two, three, four.... Five, six... seven, eight, nine, ten... An entire squadron!

"There's more, look!" Nora exclaimed. Another squadron approached from the south.

"Look, in the north!"

The sound of engines filled the air, resonated through the valleys, and bounced back with many echoes. The western squadron continued flying directly at the crater, while the northern and southern ones slowly arched to the east to pass over the settlement and drop their bombs directly after the first squadron.

"There won't be anything left of us!" Nora said. I remembered our plans to try and escape, but stayed rooted to the balcony, watching.

The airplanes were so close; I could see red stars on the underside of the wings in the bright light of the flood lights.

"Odd," Nora Said. "Mr. Bailey must have long-range weapons. The airplanes are within range, why doesn't he respond?"

"Are you in a hurry to see these birds plucked out of the air?" I asked jokingly.

"I want to see the resolution, just as you do."

That was true. I was overcome by nervous impatience – to face the inevitable, to witness the power of Mr. Bailey's defenses. We didn't have to wait long. People near the weapons sprang into action, and everything they did suggested the weapons have been fired. But I didn't hear a sound.

"These are pneumatic cannons, they use air bombs," Nora explained.

"Air bombs? What's that?" I asked, straining my eyes to see what happened when the bombs reached the airplanes. Their effect turned out to be unlike anything I expected.

"Look down – not up," Nora said. I did and saw snow dust rising from below.

"That's all?" I almost smiled.

What was happening? Snow seemed to boil in the spots where the bombs fell. Enormous clouds of steam rose up, followed by a series of sudden twisters, accompanied by terrible roaring, whistling, and screeching. A spiraling column of snow soared to the sky, started widening, growing and at the same time losing cohesion and turning into a savage winter storm. Bailey created a snowstorm! I looked at the airplanes. A curtain of white approached them with incredible speed. The leading airplane became flipped vertically, then twirled and launched backwards, like a sheet of paper propelled by a hurricane.

Second, third... In a few seconds, the entire squadron spun through the air like autumn leaves torn off a tree.

Gray mist covered the sky.

When it gradually dissipated, the sky was as deserted as before. The moon was hooked to a sharp rock, as if afraid to share the fate of the airplane, and gazed dully at the dead slopes.

I stood there in shock, breathing heavily. I felt feverish. Nora leaned against the wall, looking with widened eyes at the spot where birds of steel soared proudly only a few minutes earlier. She sighed heavily. In her words, I heard familiar hopelessness, "It's hard waging war against Mr. Bailey. Here's the result."

"It's not the end, it's the beginning!" I said, even as doubt crept into my thoughts. "Let's see what happens next."

"There's nothing to see," Nora said. "They would be mad to attempt another attack."

Nora was right – there were no new attacks. They needed time to recover from their defeat and consider the experience of the first battle.

We stayed where we were, looking toward the west.

XVII. EXPLOSIVE DEMONSTRATION

Another attack took place the next day after the appearance of the military airplanes. Nora and I were at the lab when we heard the alarm go off. We looked at each other and, in silent agreement, set down our test tubes, put on our coats, and went up to the balcony.

It was noon. The gray cloud curtain covered the sky. A solitary airplane hummed faintly somewhere above. But we couldn't see it. I understood the strategy of our pilots – to increase the altitude and use the protection of the low-lying clouds. Those in charge of our military must have decided not to dedicate large resources to this operation but use isolated strikes. Under the circumstances, it was the most sensible course of action. But, alas, it did not work.

Mr. Bailey was truly the ruler of storms. Before the airplane was directly above us, the giant fans came on and sent a powerful column of air up into the sky. This invisible battering ram punched a hole in the clouds, scattering them quickly. A bit of blue sky appeared. And the airplane? We never got to see it. All I could hear through the roaring of the storm were a few halting, struggling surges of the engine, sounding like a dying screech of a wounded eagle. The wind pushed the airplane and the clouds far off to the side.

On the same day, I discovered results of these few initial battles on the radio. Unless the exact number of casualties was concealed "for strategic considerations" as Bailey stated, the losses weren't as great as I feared. Three pilots died, six were wounded, and two airplanes crashed. The government declared it would not stop until the enemy was eliminated.

"We'll see who ends up eliminated!" Bailey said arrogantly. "They haven't sample everything I have to offer."

The aerial attacks continued over the next few days, but with the same results. The radars warned the guards of the approaching airplanes well in advance, despite the use of mufflers nearly eliminating engine noise. Every time, the airplanes were thrown far off course. The entire world now knew about Ay-Toyon's Nostril. It was "breathing out" and drawing nothing in to avoid pulling in not only the airplanes but also the bombs that could explode inside the shaft.

Finally, our pilots apparently became convinced just how impossible it was to attack the underground city from the air. They no longer came.

"Smart," Bailey said. "Too bad I had to let out so much air. But there's no war without some loss. I'll pull my air back in. They'll come back to me – they'll come crawling back and begging for the smallest breath!"

Days followed one another, filled with troubled expectation. The guards remained at their observation posts, reminding us we were at war, but otherwise life at the settlement continued as usual.

In a few days, the lull was broken by the sounds of distant cannonade. I thought it was artillery but did not hear any explosions. It happened at night, shortly before dawn. I quickly got dressed and stepped out into the corridor where I suddenly ran into Bailey.

"Your friends aren't giving up," he said angrily. "They pulled up some long-range weapons and want to destroy my city. Fools! They don't understand they are only speeding up the demise of their world. I see no need to conceal your presence here. Come to the radio station with me, I need you."

"I want to send a message," Bailey said to Luke when we came in.

Luke sat down by the transmitter. Bailey dictated, "To the Army High Command. Stop the bombing immediately. If a single shell hits Mr. Bailey's underground settlement, a world-wide disaster will occur. Enormous quantities of liquid air are stored at the settlement. Should hydrogen leak and ignite, it will combine with liquid air, which, despite the low temperature of liquid air, will produce an explosive gas with tremendously high temperature due to high oxygen concentration. The heat will instantly turn all of liquid air into gas. An explosion of incredible power will follow. The resulting hurricane will wipe cities off the face of the Earth. This will be the most unprecedented catastrophe in human history, Klimenko."

"You want the message to come from me?" I asked in surprise.

"Yes, you. Don't you want to prevent this terrible disaster? They are more likely to believe you than me. I'm not exaggerating. You've seen the stores of liquid hydrogen, the lakes of liquid air, and the piles of air-filled spheres. If you don't believe me, feel free to ask Professor Engelbrecht."

Engelbrecht might be on Bailey's side, I thought.

"I can't send this message," I replied.

"Why?"

"Because I only believe things I'd seen for myself. I know nothing of the effect of the air balls."

"Indeed! You don't believe me? Very well, I'll give you a chance. It will cost me, but it well cost your friends even more."

He turned to Luke and added, "Send the message and sign as I instructed. We don't need his agreement!"

"But I object!"

"Object all you like... Come." I remained where I was.

"Do you want me to arrest you?"

I was at his mercy. My arrest wouldn't have helped anything, whereas remaining free allowed me to interfere with Bailey. I had to obey.

The message was sent and received. The cannons remained silent for some time – apparently, high command had to contact Moscow. But the next day, the weapons came alive once again. One shell exploded at the bottom of the crater. Bailey decided he couldn't afford to take any more risks and gave orders to "teach them a lesson". Another message was sent, stating Mr. Bailey would discharge one millionth of the stored air to convince his enemy and the rest of the world, what effect a larger explosion might have.

Several barrels filled with harmless-looking shiny balls were rolled to the western slope of the crater. All trap doors were shut and locked. Bailey invited Nora and me to watch the explosion through a small window cut out in the rock and covered with glass five centimeters thick.

"See for yourself," he said," how these little beads work."

"They are just sitting there, despite the air temperature minus twelve degrees Celsius, and atmospheric pressure lower than usual."

"Did you expect them to explode immediately? We wouldn't have been able to get them outside. Engelbrecht invented a substance that slows down evaporation and delays the explosion. Wait a little..."

"But why don't you use this protective substance on all the balls?"

"Nothing will help against the heat from an exploding artillery shell. Look, it's starting!"

Indeed, I saw the balls at the very top beginning to smoke. Soon the barrels were swathed in a cloud of steam. This cloud grew with incredible speed, covering everything before us.

"It's not the explosion, not yet," Bailey said. "It's only the evaporation of the protective shell. And here..." He didn't finish.

Something cracked, boomed, and I passed out.

When I opened my eyes, I saw the sky above me covered with clouds spinning and roiling as if in a colossal whirlpool. Our observation room no longer had an outer wall. The ceiling was also gone – the gust of hurricane wind was so great not a single stone fell on us – they were carried off like straw. Nora lay next to me, and Bailey was slumped by the back wall. He had a head wound; a puddle of blood was spreading around him.

I looked at the valley and did not recognize it. Not a trace was left of the forest. The trees have been pulled out with roots and carried off somewhere else. Mountain peaks and entire chunks of the ridge have been torn off. A new valley between two mountain ridges opened before me, the vast snow desert stretching beyond. It was still buffeted by heavy winds but things were relatively quiet where we were.

I tried to sit up. My entire body ached much worse than the day I was sucked in by the fan. I looked at Bailey. His mouth hung open, his eyes were glassy. He was dead. Just as well! His death was his own doing.

I leaned over Nora and tried to wake her up. She was unharmed but unconscious. I had trouble getting her to regain consciousness. CPR was not helping. I was growing desperate when I remembered the method for restoring one's heartbeat by frequent tapping of their chest over their heart. That worked. Her pulse strengthened, and Nora finally opened her eyes.

"How are you feeling?" I asked.

"Tolerable, thank you. Where's Mr. Bailey?"

"Dead," I replied, not bothering to hide my joy. Just then, I heard wheezing, followed by Bailey's voice, "Damn it! Think I overdid it."

His hands moved over the floor.

"I can't lift my head," he said dully. "Help me."

I crawled over to Bailey, and pulled him up, leaning him against the wall. His head slumped to the side.

"Fifty thousand times atmospheric pressure. The shock wave was supposed to travel in the direction of heating. The heater was on the western side. What a contusion!" Bailey mumbled trying to determine his mistake. He groaned and closed his eyes.

A thought flashed through my mind like lightning. Mr. Bailey was at my mercy! If I... No one would know! I picked up a large rock and raised it over Bailey's head. Nora grabbed my hand and pushed it aside.

"Shame on you! Killing a sick, wounded, helpless man!" she whispered.

I was taken aback. The stone fell from my hand.

"But you..."

"Eh? What? What are you talking about?" Mr. Bailey asked opening his right eye.

"You must be taken to your room, we'll call for help," Nora said, rubbing her cheeks, white with cold. "Mr. Klimenko, get some help."

I hesitated. But at that moment, William pushed his way through the broken door. His clothes were torn, his face was covered in bruises and scrapes. Clearly, he too had a bad time of it. Two other servants showed up after him. He picked up Bailey, maneuvered his body through the ruined door with some difficulty, and carried him off.

Nora surveyed the scene of destruction.

"This is terrible!" she said.

"Soon, you'll regret your kindness."

"Perhaps, but I couldn't have acted otherwise," the girl replied. "It was beyond me."

XVIII. BAILEY TAKES OFF HIS MASK

Nora ended up taking care of the injured Bailey. His condition was fairly serious. He was suffering from headaches. At times, he was delirious. Nora stayed with him the first few nights, never leaving his side.

"How is he?" I asked Nora every time we met, secretly hoping Bailey didn't survive.

"No changes," Nora replied and, seeing my disappointed, added awkwardly. "You probably disapprove of my weakness, but I told you – this is beyond me. I can't…"

"How is his mood?"

"This morning Mr. Bailey woke up and said, 'I earned myself a decent bruise, but bruises of my enemies will be far greater.'."

Bailey was right. His "demonstration" had caused great damage. For thousands of kilometers to the west, where the main power of the explosion was directed, the country was in a sorry state. It was as if a giant razor slid over the globe, shaving off centuries-old forests, villages, cities… Rivers flooded, finishing what the storm had started. Those who didn't die from the wind ended up drowning. Corpses of people and animals were scattered everywhere. Entire houses were thrown to the tops of mountains or into lakes, sometimes hundreds of kilometers away.

The area between the sixtieth and seventieth latitudes sustained the most damage. Fortunately for the heavier populated areas of Europe, the epicenter of the explosion was far removed. The Ural Mountains also weakened the hurricane somewhat. Ufa, Sverdlovsk, Perm, and other cities located closer to the Ural Range suffered less than the Volga Region.

The wind seemed to make a great leap over the Urals and crashed onto Samara, Nizhny Novgorod, Vologda, as well as Moscow, Riga, and Warsaw. Poland, Germany, north of France, and England looked as if they had been hit by a terrible earthquake. Then the storm swept over the Atlantic Ocean, drowned many ships, hit the eastern seaboard of the United States, wreaked havoc across Canada and the US, and rushed across the Pacific Ocean toward Japan, thus circling the entire globe as it arrived to the deserts of Asia. One stormy night, our mountain shook as if feverish under the onslaught of the eastern wind. Gradually slowing down, the storm traveled around the globe four times. Its periodic gusts were felt for a long time.

It was a good lesson! The world shuddered in terror.

The fairy tale about communists preparing to suffocate the world collapsed onto itself. Bailey's name was everywhere, after he sent a telegram to the entire world, inviting the governments to acknowledge his rule and surrender their weapons. Countries hit the hardest were in a state of panic. The media demanded a truce, suggesting the governments must begin negotiations with Mr. Bailey immediately.

Only the Soviet Union declared it would not lay down its arms until the enemy was defeated. This decision caused an explosion of outrage in German, English, French, and American media. If USSR was going to be stubborn, the European nations and USA could make peace with Mr. Bailey without it. If USSR resisted, the entire world would turn against it.

Indeed, soon enough Mr. Bailey received a telegram from the governments of Germany, France, Great Britain, and United States, offering him to outline his conditions.

Bailey didn't delay. His ultimatum included three points:

1. Global establishment of capitalist dictatorship.
2. Physical extermination of all communists and socialists.
3. Mr. Bailey retaining monopoly on air sales, as a guarantee providing stability to the political system he established.

Finally, Bailey revealed his true persona. I still doubt whether his story about trading with Mars was true. But his Earth-bound goals became clear when I found out about the ultimatum. Bailey pursued his own social and political agenda – he wanted to enslave the lower classes for eternity, forcing them into working for the right to breathe, literally!

Capitalist government found Mr. Bailey's conditions more than acceptable. But the working classes reacted to the ultimatum with protests. Their employers hoped to handle the resistance fairly quickly. "Anyone against us will be left without air," they retorted, defending a truce with Bailey.

The world was facing another, terrible bloodshed. Only two days after the ultimatum, the radical media cynically stated any coup by the workers would be "completely bloodless", implying they would simply suffocate.

I told the news to Nora. She listened to me quietly, only her lips trembled.

"This cannot continue," she said after a pause. "I must talk to my father today. Come to our balcony at midnight. I'll tell you what I find out from him."

In the evening, Luke came to visit me. He was uncommonly glum. He didn't even offer me a game of chess. Instead, he paced around the room and cussed.

"Is something bothering you, Luke?" I asked him.

"Sure I am," he mumbled. "I hope Mr. Bailey blows up along with all your friends!"

"What's the matter, Luke?"

Luke stood with his legs spread, his arms crossed, and said dramatically, "There isn't a drop of gin left in the settlement!"

"What?" I exclaimed in surprised. "Are we running out of things?"

"We are!" Luke snapped. "There's no gin, and soon there won't be anything else except frozen meat." He paused, then continued, "This is no time for secrets! We won't get out of this mousetrap anyway. We used to have things delivered by plane. Mr. Bailey always maintained some connection with the outside world. Even with all his wealth, he couldn't have created and maintained this enterprise on his own. Mr. Bailey is not alone. He has many allies. And they continued supporting him and refilling our stores. But now we are in a blockade. Your pilots managed to establish such a rigid boundary, even a crow couldn't get through, let alone an airplane – storm or no storm! We have already sent three desperate telegrams to our allies in Great Britain and received the same answer every time, 'Cannot get to you. Wait until the truce.' Wait!" Like concluded angrily. "It's easy for them to say. What about me?"

What Luke said was a kind of revelation for me. In one respect, Bailey turned out to be stronger than I thought. Apparently, he was not a solitary dissident but was leading a large conspiracy! The world's entire capital could be at Bailey's disposal. Dubbing him "the air merchant" was nothing more than a clever trick to avoid the anger of the lower classes against those in power. As it was, it appeared a single maniac or villain took control of the air supply, and the rest were simply forced to accept his conditions!

On the other hand, based on what Luke told me, Bailey's own position, and that of his underground city was nearly catastrophic. Should the settlement fall, the entire conspiracy would fall with it. No one in the world knew that. Our government did not know. There was a reason why foreign nations were in such a rush to make truce with Mr. Bailey. The next few days were going to be critical. Any means to the goal were acceptable. If Nora didn't have it in her to finish off Mr. Bailey, I was going to do it!

The news Luke brought me was so important, I decided to reward him, and pulled from under my bed a bottle of gin I stashed away a week earlier.

At the sight of the coveted bottle, Luke growled and attacked it like a wild animal. He started drinking straight from the bottle and pulled away only after he had downed half. He wiped his mouth, carefully capped the bottle, put it in his pocket, thanked me, and left.

XIX.   HANDS UNTIED

I looked at the clock. It was ten minutes to midnight – time to go to the balcony.

Nora wasn't there yet. Lilac-green bouquets blossomed in the sky against the backdrop of cheerfully sweeping yellow and blue bands. Pale orange drapes danced over the horizon. The sky was gloriously illuminated that night. Oxygen and neon spectral lines joined those of nitrogen and helium in a merry quadrille.

The door creaked behind me. I turned. Nora!

She was as pale as a frozen corpse. Without a word, the girl walked up to me, put her hands on my shoulders, raised her face to mine, and kissed me. My breath caught from this unexpected gesture.

"Nora!" I exclaimed quietly.

She stepped away from me and said, "Everything will be alright now. I need to go downstairs to the liquid air lake. Father asked me to go," she said meaningfully, "and Mr. Bailey. Come with me."

"Nora! Nora! What did you father say? What do you mean? Why are you so pale?"

Everything I wanted to tell Nora went clear out of my head. The girl's behavior was so unusual, and she spoke so imperiously, I followed her like a robot. She walked quickly. Several times I called out to her and tried speaking to her, but the girl only walked faster.

We entered the room where the suits for visiting the absolute cold caves were stored.

"Please help me dress quickly," Nora said, "and don't ask anything. You'll know everything soon."

I had to obey. We quickly put on the suits, took an elevator down, silently passed through the series of doors, and entered the underground cavern. The blue liquid air lake smoked slightly. The cold lamps shone brightly.

We walked along the shore of the lake. Nora slowed down and stumbled several times, as if her legs no longer supported her. I took her arm, but she pulled away and said to me, "Let's keep going.

"Why?"

"We have to."

I obediently took a few steps forward and suddenly heard a weak cry. I turned to look and shuddered in terror.

"What are you doing?!" I screamed. But it was too late.

Nora opened her suit exposing her head and chest to the cold of minus two hundred seventy-three degrees Celsius, which would kill her instantly. I ran up to the girl and, with shaking hands, tried to pull the hood over her head and zip the suit over her chest. Nora's body instantly became covered in frost and became hard as steel. Even her eyes, which remained open, were covered with a film of frost, and a tiny bit of ice fell from her parted, smiling lips – Nora's last breath. Some of the frost fell from her body and floated to the floor like snow.

"Nora! Nora! What have you done?" I shouted, half-mad.

I stood before the girl's ice statue, not knowing what to do. Suddenly, I saw a frost-covered rectangular object at her feet. I picked it up, wiped off the frost, and saw it was a letter.

I looked back at Nora and saw the frost descended further, covering her entire figure. I decided to take her to the "pantheon" and place her onto the pedestal Mr. Bailey reserved for me. I thought it would be the best way to honor the poor girl. I put my arm around her frozen body and tried picking it up. But the girl's feet were frozen to the ground with the ice formed by the escaping warmth of her body. I tried again and suddenly felt Nora's body crack and split into several pieces. I was startled and let go, causing the top part of the body slide to the side, held up only by the suit. Several pieces fell out, like shards of a broken statue. Within seconds, Nora, a warm, living Nora turned into a statue, more fragile and delicate than porcelain!

I was deeply saddened and shocked by this transformation. Finally pulling the girl's feet off the ground, I hoisted the porcelain remains onto my shoulders, took them to the "pantheon", and placed them on the pedestal. Alas, I could only restore a bust portrait of Nora. Having carefully cleared her face from the store and looked for the last time at the lips that had only just kissed me, I left the gloomy cave, went up, rushed to my room, carefully warmed up and dried the letter, and started reading.

"Dear friend!" Nora wrote. "Forgive me for subjecting you to these unpleasant minutes. I was afraid I couldn't do what I had to do without you. Your presence supported me.

"I spoke to my father and made him confess everything. I now know, what forced him to work with Mr. Bailey.

"Mr. Bailey deceived my father. He lured him to the settlement, having promised to let him go a year later. But when a year passed, Bailey told my father he would not set him free. If my father disobeyed, neither one of us would have left here alive. My father loves me very much. He could not risk my life and stayed with Mr. Bailey. But he found it hard admitting to me he was imprisoned. That was why he assured me he stayed because of work.

"Thus, I was tying him down. Because of me, my father had to participate in this terrible enterprise.

"One time, you reproached me for not being like my revolutionary ancestor, Engelbrecht the miner. Yes, I must admit I don't have his will power and his boundless energy. Centuries and generations of descendants must have diluted his iron-clad character. I could not kill Mr. Bailey. For I long time, I could not ask my father the fateful question about his complicity in a crime. But I wish to die as a worthy great-granddaughter of Engelbrecht, the miner. That is all I can do. Now my father is free. It's hard for me to write to him. Would you please pass on to him my words? 'Father, your hands are no longer tied. Act as Engelbrecht, the miner would have acted.' Farewell. Nora."

I re-read the letter several times. Poor Nora! She acted too quickly. If only I had a chance to tell her what I found out from Luke, perhaps she would have stayed alive. And... she loved me. But it was all over now. Not everything in Nora's letter was clear to me. Perhaps, her father would explain.

It was morning. I went to see Professor Engelbrecht.

He was at his office, absorbed in his formulas. When he saw me, the professor looked up from his papers and asked me calmly, "Have you seen my daughter?"

"Something terrible has happened to your daughter... to Miss Eleonora," I said. Engelbrecht blanched.

"What happened? Tell me!"

I quietly placed Nora's letter on his desk. The professor's hands visibly shook, but he tried to regain control. Having read the letter, he looked at me and said quietly, "What happened?"

I told her what took place in the absolute cold cave. I was almost calm.

Engelbrecht lowered his head and covered his face. He sat that way for several minutes. I didn't break the silence. When he finally looked up, I did not recognize him – his face changed and aged.

Engelbrecht rose with difficulty, swayed, and sat back down.

"I killed her—"

Suddenly he slammed his fist on the desk, and his eyes flashed with anger.

"Bailey killed her!"

The spirit of Engelbrecht's ancestor seemed to come alive within him.

"Come with me to this scoundrel!" he shouted.

"One question, professor," I said.

"Quickly..."

"Miss Eleonora wrote that, according to you, Bailey threatened to kill you and her if you decided to leave. Meanwhile, she said he did not hold her back."

"It was Mr. Bailey's game, a psychological game. He knew Nora would not leave without me. I had to sustain in my daughter the illusion she was free. Had she known of her captivity, our situation would have become even more complicated. She would have been miserable."

"What if she decided to leave after all?"

"Mr. Bailey would not have let her go."

"But why didn't you... kill Bailey?"

"I have thought about it more than once. But killing Mr. Bailey would not have changed the situation. Mr. Bailey is but one of the links in a chain of crime. You know who constitutes

134

the majority of the settlement's population, with the exception of a few Yakut workers? The sons of bankers and magnates! They would not have let me out, if I killed Bailey. They would have killed Nora and me. Or they might have killed me and left her alive. But what would have happened to her? Poor girl, she was right – my hands were tied because of her. But had I known Nora would do this... In any case, it's too late to talk about it now. Yes, Mr. Bailey doesn't joke about such things. I would have been dealt with the same way as my colleagues who perished on board the *Arctic*. They were killed because they wouldn't obey Mr. Bailey."

The professor started searching through one of the desk drawers.

"Damn it, where is my revolver?"

I wanted to say Nora looked for it and couldn't find it, but kept mum.

"Fine, we'll do without. Come, Mr. Klimenko."

"What do you plan to do?" I asked.

"Have a heart-to-heart with Mr. Bailey..."

Our visit to Bailey didn't start very successfully. He was in his armchair, surrounded by his closest associates – at least ten of them.

Seeing this, Engelbrecht frowned, but it was too late to back out.

"Ah, my dear professor, how appropriate!" Bailey said. "I was just about to send for you. We are holding a small military council. My head doesn't work so well..."

Bailey paused and ran his fingers through the shiny beads on a platter in front of him. The beads were Engelbrecht's latest invention – compressed air enclosed in special shells. Contained this way, the air did not evaporate at room temperature and could be safely transported. Only a sudden increase in temperature could cause an explosion. Bailey accelerated preparations for air export, believing the truce on his terms a foregone conclusion.

"Yes, my head..." Mr. Bailey continued. "My head is not alright. I start talking and suddenly find myself saying nonsense. But it will pass. Sit down, sir..."

Bailey did not offer me a seat. He merely glanced at me but did not ask me to leave.

"I refuse to work. You may no longer consider me one of your staff," Engelbrecht said, still standing.

"You refuse?!" Bailey asked, and his face darkened. "What do you mean, sir?"

"It means what I said."

"All that matters here is what I say," Bailey replied angrily. "You forget Mr. Engelbrecht. If you don't immediately..."

"Enough!" Engelbrecht shouted suddenly. "I don't want to stay in this gang of thieves anymore!"

"This is mutiny. Do you know what you are facing?"

"Scum!" Engelbrecht roared. "You killed my daughter, you filled the world with terror, you... you..." Engelbrecht rushed at Bailey and tried throttling him.

No one expected this from Engelbrecht. For a few moments, Bailey's cronies remained motionless and then attacked the professor. I rushed to his help. Unimaginable chaos ensued. Engelbrecht was an uncommonly strong man. My fists worked ceaselessly too. But we were outnumbered, and our enemies overwhelmed us. Bailey hid behind the desk, surrounded himself with a barricade of chairs, and oversaw the battle from there.

He became delirious from anxiety and screamed obsessively, "Away! To Mars! To the Moon! End of the world! A hundred thousand pounds per gram!"

Engelbrecht shoved aside his opponents trying to push his way through to Bailey and wheezed, "I'll kill you... I'll rip you to pieces!"

We were growing weaker. I shouted to Engelbrecht, "Back off! Retreat, or we are dead..."

Engelbrecht had regained his senses somewhat. He looked around and saw the situation was hopeless. Three of our opponents were sprawled on the floor, but the rest armed themselves with chairs and were ready to attack us again.

Two of them pulled out automatic pistols.

Engelbrecht and I retreated toward the door, putting up a hell of a fight, and ran down the corridor, our enemies hot on our heels. We turned around the corner, jumped into an elevator, and went down a floor. In a few moments we found ourselves not far from the outlet tube. The access to it was blocked.

"Quickly! Quickly!" Engelbrecht shouted, pulling me along, since he knew the layout of the settlement better than I did.

XX.   DOOMED

We ran into a cave adjacent to the tube and quickly closed the door.

This was an unfinished space, eventually intended for liquid air storage. The cooling elements were not yet installed, and the temperature in the cave was tolerable. Presently, it was used for storing spare wagonettes and tools. There was no lighting.

"Pull up the wagonettes!" Engelbrecht commanded, blocking the entrance.

We rolled the wagonettes to the metal door, piled pick axes, shovels, and whatever else we could find in the darkness on top. The only door was now securely barricaded.

"Well," the professor said, once we were done. "We can hold out here for a long time.

We heard muffled footsteps of our pursuers from beyond the door.

Soon we heard pounding. We were silent. The pounding stopped after some time, and all went quiet. We didn't know whether our enemies realized it would be impossible to open the door or changed their plan of attack, but we were glad of this respite. We were barely standing from fatigue. Engelbrecht climbed into a wagonette and stretched.

"That was stupid," he said. "I couldn't stand it. Such is my temper. I tolerated it all for a long time, and then exploded."

He paused.

"Do you believe me to be Mr. Bailey's accomplice?" he finally spoke up.

"But you couldn't have..." I tried to comfort him.

"No, I could. I could have averted the catastrophe and saved countless lives by sacrificing myself and my daughter. Such sacrifice would have been difficult. But it would have been better to lose two than thousands, wouldn't it?"

"What use is self-flagellation?" I shrugged.

"It's not self-flagellation. Your opinion is important to me. My daughter did not write her last letter to me – she wrote it to you. She loved you, I saw as much..."

I said nothing. Engelbrecht, this big, strong man, was clearly torn and could no longer hide his grief.

"Don't think too badly of me," he said. "Whatever is my guilt before humankind, I have been cruelly punished for it. I spent many sleepless nights looking for a way out. I was looking for a way to disable Mr. Bailey's factory, but in such a way as to not cause an accident. I had you and Nora working on that very thing lately. Your conscience can rest – you were not working for Bailey but against him. And the experiments were very successful. They were almost finished. If only Nora waited... Poor girl! But I couldn't solve the problem for a long time. There were days when I felt nothing but desperation. And then I thought – today, it all must end. I shall kill Nora, then Bailey, then myself. But whenever Nora walked in, glowing with health and youth... Ah!" Engelbrecht sighed heavily. "I couldn't do it. Then Nora stopped trusting me. Didn't I see the terrible question in her eyes? Was her father a criminal? Her father – the man she loved so much and whose honesty she never questioned!"

Engelbrecht suddenly rose and stepped toward me.

"My little girl is gone. I am having a very hard time of it... But you know, a tremendous weight fell from my shoulders! The time of my 'split personality' is over. You and I are doomed.

But I am not thinking about myself. I regret only one thing – I failed to strangle the scoundrel. Apparently, they are going to try and starve us to death. Fortunately, they cannot freeze us. Although, what does it matter? Didn't Nora freeze herself?"

The girl's death had a great impact on me too. I loved her and lost her just as I discovered she loved me too. But I didn't carry the same burden as Engelbrecht did. Besides, I was young, and my mood was not as hopeless as his. I wanted to live.

"Tell me, is there no way out of here?" I asked Engelbrecht.

The professor was too absorbed in his gloomy thoughts, and my question didn't reach him right away.

"Get out?" he finally repeated. "There is, but it won't be easy. This is an outer wall."

"What's the problem, then?" I said. "We have pick axes Of course, it's completely dark here, but we can work even in the dark."

"We can," Engelbrecht replied listlessly. "But we'll starve before we get through the rock. It's a waste of time. Lie down and calmly wait for your death, as I am doing."

I was not planning to calmly wait for death. Once I rested, I rose, felt around for a pick axe, and walked up to the wall.

Ringing strikes echoed in the darkness.

"Not there, move to the left," I heard Engelbrecht say. "The wall is thinner in that spot."

I took a few steps to the left and continued working.

Tired, I sat down and heard Engelbrecht's wheezing and clanging of metal – the professor hopped off the wagonette.

"I am too tired, down to my soul, to pound at the rock for the sake of saving my own life. But you are young and will yet find your happiness. I must help you for Nora's sake."

There was more metallic clanging as Engelbrecht picked out a pick axe.

"No one cuts through rocks this way," I heard professor's voice near me. "Step aside. Let me show you how the old miner, Engelbrecht did it."

I heard smooth, powerful strikes.

We worked for several hours. At some point, I threw down my pick axe in utter exhaustion, but I heard the pounding of "the old miner, Engelbrecht" for a long time in that vast cavern. The echo responded loudly.

"That's enough for today," Engelbrecht finally said.

He also dropped his pick axe. But before we settled for the night, we dragged the Wagonettes away from the door and set them onto the rails in a row, going across the entire cave. The first wagonettes pressed against the door, and the last one – against the opposite wall.

"Here. If we pile tools and rocks onto the wagonettes, devil, himself couldn't open this door."

Finally, completely exhausted, we lay down and fell sound asleep.

I woke up from cold. I was hungry. I heard Engelbrecht's long yawn in the darkness.

"Awake?" I asked.

"For a while. I'm hungry, but we've no choice – we have to get to work without breakfast."

He picked up the pick axe. At first, his strikes were uncertain and uneven, but then Engelbrecht became absorbed in work with the same energy as before. I too picked up my pick axe.

Hunger was palpable now, weakening us. We made increasingly frequent stops to rest. Time passed endlessly slowly. The rock seemed harder than it was the day before. Finally, I threw down my pick axe in helpless desperation and dropped onto a pile of rocks like a sack. Engelbrecht continued working for some time, but then his strikes faded away too.

"This is bad," he said glumly. "We won't last very long at this rate, and we're only a third of the way through the rock. We are not working very efficiently. We should go for a smaller opening and take turns."

Another day passed, assuming we weren't mistaken about the time. We tried sleeping again, huddled in the same wagonette to stay warm. The cold grew stronger and more torturous. I couldn't sleep. My stomach clenched from hunger spasms. My feet felt cold, my head was burning, and my entire body ached. As hard as I tried fighting dark thoughts, they didn't leave me alone. I was losing hope we would ever make it out of there. I wanted to talk to Engelbrecht, but he was very quiet, possibly asleep. I felt bad about waking him.

Giving up all hope to fall asleep, I rose, made my way to the hole we were beating through the wall, and started measuring the distance we had covered so far. Rocks rolled from under my feet rumbling.

"Who's there?" I heard Engelbrecht's voice.

"It's me. Aren't you asleep?"

"No," the professor replied. "Damn thoughts... And it's cold... Let's warm up." Engelbrecht got up and picked up the pick axe.

"Damn, it's gotten heavier!" he cursed. I heard the pounding, followed by silence and a heavy sigh.

"I can't," Engelbrecht said. "I can't even pick up the axe. I have to!" And he went back to work so hard sparks flew.

It was the last energy surge. The pick axe flew off to the side and Engelbrecht sprawled on the pile of rocks.

"Rest, I'll step in," I said, resuming work.

I did even worse than before. I thought I was swinging as hard as I could, but my pick axe only scratched the rock, breaking off small bits. At that rate, we wouldn't make it through the rock even in ten years! We were bound to starve to death sooner than that...

Perhaps I fell asleep or passed out, pick axe in hand. I don't know how long this continued. Maybe I lay there an entire day or maybe a few minutes. I couldn't tell for certain, whether it was in a dream or in reality, when I got back to work several times, pounded with savage desperation, and fell back down. From time to time I felt unbearable surges of hunger. But gradually this sensation became duller. I was beginning to fall into a stupor. Time stopped, and I could no longer tell how many days passed since we had locked ourselves in this mouse trap. I fell deeper and deeper into the dark abyss of oblivion. The thought of death flickered by occasionally, but it no longer worried me.

Numb indifference was sucking me in like a swamp. But not all of my critical emotions were gone yet. I remember watching with some interest the process of dying taking place within me. There was a certain rhythm about it. Periods of nearly comatose condition gave way to clearer thoughts and feelings, as if I gathered the last few bits of my life force to brighten my consciousness the last few times. Only consciousness could find a way out and save the dying body. And the body was surrendering its last resources, the last fluttering of cells to my brain – the last hope for salvation.

During one such interval I heard weak, distant strikes of a pick axe.

Engelbrecht must be at it again. Can it be that someone starving to death might also be going deaf? I wondered. Or is it delirium?

"Is that you, Professor?" I asked Engelbrecht.

"I was just about to ask you the same thing," he replied in a weak voice I heard with perfect clarity.

"I am not going deaf then, and it's not a hallucination," I thought out loud. "What does it mean? Who is pounding? Where?"

"I'd been thinking about this for a few minutes or hours," Engelbrecht replied. "I thought it was you, and I was also going deaf. The sounds are coming from the opening we made – I'm right next to it." After a pause, he continued, "Apparently, Mr. Bailey is in a hurry to finish us off, and he gave orders to break the wall. He's all about law and order and probably wants to try us properly to freeze and later put in the pantheon."

We paused, listening. The sounds strengthened and came closer. Then they stopped and were replaced by a new sound – the screeching of a turning drill.

"They're using an auger," Engelbrecht said calmly. "They are bound to get here pretty quickly."

The new danger seemed to restore our energies. I can't say I was afraid of death, since I was already approaching it, but these new sounds broke the monotony of our life and the rhythm of our gradual dying. We both became completely conscious.

"What are we going to do?" I asked.

"We'll face our enemies and die in battle, like real men," Engelbrecht replied.

I smiled sarcastically, without having to worry Engelbrecht might see me.

"Can you raise an arm?" I asked.

"I have enough strength to drop a rock on the head of the first person who sticks it in here," he said. "Crawl over here."

We crept to the edge of the small opening we made and settled on each side, keeping sharp-edged rocks close at hand. The monotonous screeching of the drill was making me drowsy, but I was battling it as hard as I could. When the sounds appeared right next to us, my sleepiness disappeared. I perked up like a cat preparing to catch a mouse.

"A few more minutes, and they'll be here," Engelbrecht whispered.

At that moment I knew what was filling us with strength – the hatred of our enemies!

The drill squealed, the wall cracked, and small stones poured toward us. Squealing and screeching were replaced by buzzing. A hole appeared in the thin wall separating us from the enemies, then another... Strikes of a pick axe. The hole became large enough to let through a person. I figured as much, since the drill and the pick axes stopped their work, and I heard rustling in the dark that could only come from someone crawling through the opening. Straining our weakened muscles, the professor and I raised the rocks. I listened to every sound. Closer, closer... Even closer...

Now! I thought and swung my arm higher. Suddenly, the rock fell from my hands at the sound of a familiar whisper...

XXI. "MERCHANT WENT BUST"

"Awful dark, though..."

"Nikola!" I shouted.

"Oh! Comrade Klimenko!" he replied. I felt a furry glove shaking the same hand that almost smashed his head.

"How did you get here?"

"Awful loud!" Nikola said and, turning back, addressed someone standing beyond the opening, "Come on in, comrades. All good. We came save you," he continued, addressing the professor, "kill merchant Bailey."

"Who is 'we'?"

"Red Army came. Oh!"

"But why did you decide to drill the wall of this shaft? Did you know I was here?"

"Not know. You said new shaft good to get into town," Nikola replied.

I remembered nothing of the sort. Only a long time ago, when thinking back about our nightly discussions planning the escape, I recalled pointing out that way as the most convenient for getting into the underground settlement. I didn't expect Nikola to be so industrious and retentive. We ended up in the shaft by accident and, happily, met with the rescue party.

Nikola rushed to tell me what happened. Our government kept making plans for storming the underground city. When the aerial attacks failed, and bombardment was proven impossible, the army engineers took over. It's been decided to dig under the settlement. The task was made easier by deep snow covering the entire crater. The sappers made trenches in it and got all the way to the rack. It took them three weeks, first using hand tools through the snow, then making

147

their way through an underground tunnel. The choice was made very well. Nikola had worked in this cave many times. He knew no one lived there and it could be accessed unnoticed at night, when there were no workers.

While Nikola told me his story, soldiers climbed into the cave through the opening, one after another.

"No one will see, we need light," Nikola said, and an electric flashlight appeared in his hand. "Mighty nice thing!" he said. "Click and on! Ay-ay-ay!" he continued when the beam of light hit my face. "Too thin. Hungry long time. Is this friend? Eat!" Nikola opened his backpack and started feeding Engelbrecht and me.

Once full, I told Nikola and the unit commander what had happened to us. We discussed the plan of further actions. It was morning, and the commander decided we would do better to wait until the following night to catch them by surprise.

We tried being as quiet as possible to avoid attracting attention. We set a small fire. Nikola made tea and continued feeding us. The day passed quickly in conversation and planning. At six in the evening, the commander appointed several guards and ordered the rest to get some sleep before the "mission". Fed and warmed by the fire, I fell soundly asleep, and when Nikola woke me up in the middle of the night, I felt refreshed and energetic. My legs were still a little weak, but this was not going to stop me. I wanted to participate in the raid.

We carefully rolled away the wagonettes and unblocked the exit. I hoped the door wasn't locked! One of the soldiers pulled the handle, and the door moved. Engelbrecht and I presented so little danger to Bailey's "army", he didn't consider it necessary to lock us in. We would have died on other side of the door.

The commander gave an order, and the soldiers moved along the corridor, their weapons at the ready. The corridor was empty. The first time we encountered someone was by the elevator. The guard on duty had dosed off, woke up as we approached, and tried to raise alarm, but the commander pointed a gun at him.

"Stop right there, brother!" he said in Russian but expressively enough to be understood. The guard surrendered. We took the elevator to the first floor. When the last soldier joined us, someone's shadow flickered around the turn. We had only a few minutes before someone raised alarm all around the settlement. We sped up and ran toward Bailey's study.

The door was unlocked. I pulled it open and rushed into the room.

Bailey was still up. He was sitting in an armchair running his fingers through the platter of "air" beads. His head was bandaged.

When he saw me leading a squad of armed soldiers, Bailey's eyes opened wide. His jaw dropped. He leaned back and watched us with obvious horror.

"Mr. Bailey?" the commander asked.

"That's him," I said. The commander stepped toward Bailey.

"You are under arrest."

Bailey's face twisted. His eyes widened even more and flared up with the fire of madness. He was about to have one of the fits he has been suffering lately ever since the accident.

"A-a-a-a-ah!" he screamed wildly. "Bolsheviks! A-a-a! Here? Everywhere?! There's no escape! Are you going to take away my air?"

His crooked fingers sunk into his treasure – the beads, and he suddenly picked up several, lifted them with an effort, put them in his mouth and swallowed.

Engelbrecht was the first to understand what was about to happen. He grabbed Bailey by the collar and dragged him to the exit.

"What are you trying to do with him?" the commander asked, not yet realizing the danger.

Bailey was delirious and tried fighting Engelbrecht.

"Upstairs! Quick! Help me – he's twice as heavy!" Engelbrecht shouted desperately.

Nikola, two soldiers, and I picked up Bailey, dragged him along the corridor, threw him into the elevator, and went up to the balcony, where Nora and I spent so much time talking, enjoying the northern lights, and breathing the "air vitamins".

Bailey continued screaming and tried to pull away from us.

Suddenly, I noticed a cloud of cold white vapor bursting from Bailey's mouth. His body started swelling, especially the chest. The heat of his stomach melted the beads. The air started evaporated, and Bailey was going through the same thing as a deep-sea fish dragged to the surface of the ocean – his inner pressure was greater than the atmospheric pressure and was expanding his body. Another moment and...

But Engelbrecht decided not to wait. He grabbed Mr. Bailey and threw him over the railing.

In the air, Bailey's body expanded even more. Steam poured from his mouth as if from an open locomotive valve. Before Bailey reached the snowy slope, he exploded. The beads must have fully evaporated. In a cloud of white steam, I saw Bailey's arms and legs, torn from his body and flying in different directions. Within moments, the white cloud turned into air, creating a shock wave and pushing us toward the wall. I managed to remain standing and looked down. Only Bailey's head reached the snow surface. The rest of his body was torn to the smallest pieces and carried off who knows where.

We stood motionless for a few minutes, shocked by this incredible death. Nikola was the first to break the silence.

"Merchant went bust," he said.

Indeed, "merchant went bust" along with his entire air-processing enterprise!

***

The soldiers handled the underground settlement contingent very quickly and used the radio station to inform the world of the victory.

At the same time, Engelbrecht slowly and carefully raised the temperature in the underground caverns, simultaneously lowering the pressure. All the openings, pipes, and trap doors were open. Cold white vapor flowed from them turning into life-giving air. Life was returning to Earth.

Ay-Toyon's nostril was breathing out.

ABOUT THE AUTHOR

Alexander Romanovich Belyaev was born in 1884 in Smolensk, in the family of a Russian Orthodox minister. His sister Nina and brother Vasily both died young and tragically.

Following the wishes of his father, Alexander graduated the local seminary but decided not to become a minister. On the contrary, he graduated a passionate atheist. After the seminary he entered a law school in Yaroslavl. When his father died unexpectedly, Alexander had to find ways to make ends meet including tutoring, creating theater sets and playing violin in a circus orchestra.

Fortunately, his law studies did not go to waste. As soon as Belyaev graduated the law school, he established a private practice in his home town of Smolensk and soon acquired a reputation of a talented and shrewd attorney. He took advantage of the better income to travel, acquire a very respectable art collection and create a large library. Belyaev felt so secure, financially, that he got married and left his law practice to write full-time.

At the age of thirty-five Belyaev was faced with the most serious trial of his life. He became ill with Plevritis which, after an unsuccessful treatment attempt, developed into spinal tuberculosis and leg paralysis. His wife left him, unwilling to be tied to a sick man. Belyaev spent six years in bed, three of which – in a full-torso cast. Fortunately, the other two women in his life – his mother and his old nanny – refused to give up on him. They helped seek out specialists who could help him and took him away from the dismal climate of central Russia to Yalta – a famous Black Sea resort.

153

While at the hospital in Yalta, Belyaev started writing poetry. He also determined that, while he could not do much with his body, he had to do something with his mind. He read all he could find by Jules Verne, H.G. Wells and by the famous Russian scientist Tsiolkovsky. He studied languages, medicine, biology, history, and technical sciences.

No one had a clear idea how, but in 1922 Belyaev finally overcame his illness and returned to normal life and work. To cut the cost of living, Belyaev moved his family from the expensive Yalta to Moscow and took up law once again. At the same time, he put all the things he learned during the long years of his illness to use, by weaving them into fascinating adventure and science fiction plots. His works appeared more and more frequently in scientific magazines, quickly earning him the title of "Soviet Jules Verne".

After successfully publishing several full-length novels, he moved his family to St. Petersburg (then Leningrad) and once again became a full-time writer. Sadly, the cold damp climate had caused a relapse in Belyaev's health. Unwilling to jeopardize his family's finances by moving to yet another resort town, he compromised by moving them somewhat further south, where the cost of living was still reasonable – to Kiev.

The family didn't get to enjoy the better climes for long. In 1930 the writer's six-year old daughter died of meningitis, his second daughter contracted rickets, and his own illness once again grew worse.

The following years were full of ups and downs. There was the meeting with one of Belyaev's heroes – H.G. Wells n 1934. There was the parting of ways with the magazine Around the World after eleven years of collaboration. There was the controversial article Cinderella about the dismal state of science fiction at the time.

Shortly before the Great Patriotic War (June 22, 1941 – May 9, 1945), Alexander Romanovich went through yet another surgery and could not evacuate when the war began. The town of Pushkin, a St. Petersburg suburb, where Belyaev and his family lived, became occupied by the German troops. Belyaev died of hunger in January, 1942. A German general and four soldiers took his body away and buried it somewhere. It was highly irregular for the members of the German military to bury a dead Soviet citizen. When asked about it, the general explained that he used to enjoy Belyaev's books as a boy, and considered it his duty to bury him properly.

The exact place of Belyaev's burial is unknown to this day. After the war, the Kazan cemetery of the town of Pushkin received a commemorative stele as the sign of remembrance and respect for the great author.

ABOUT THE TRANSLATOR

Maria K. is the pen name of Maria Igorevna Kuroshchepova – a writer, translator, and blogger of Russian-Ukrainian decent. Maria came to the United States in 1994 as an impressionable 19-year old exchange student. She received her Bachelors and Masters degrees in engineering from Rochester Institute of Technology (Rochester, NY).

Maria covers a wide range of topics from travel and fashion to politics and social issues. Her science fiction and fantasy works include *Limited Time for Tomato Soup*, *The SHIELD*, *The Elemental Tales* and others.

A non-fiction and science fiction writer in her own right, Maria is also a prolific translator of less-known works of Russian and Soviet literature into English. Her most prominent translations include her grandfather Vasily Kuznetsov's Siege of Leningrad journals titled *The Ring of Nine*, and *Thais of Athens* – a historic novel by Ivan Yefremov. Both works quickly made their way into the top 100 Kindle publications in their respective categories and continue attracting consistent interest and acclaim from readers.

CPSIA information can be obtained
at www.ICGtesting.com
Printed in the USA
LVHW080811010822
724834LV00001B/93

9 781533 044372